SNOW HAPPENS

ALASKA COZY MYSTERY #3

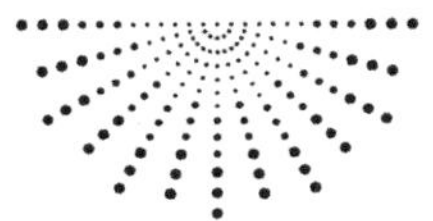

WENDY MEADOWS

Printed in the United States of America

CHAPTER ONE

Diamond Lake was shaped like its namesake, a beautiful, priceless rock. The frozen lake appeared to be snuggled down into a mysterious dream as it cuddled under a blanket of snow, surrounded by white trees and huddled under a dark gray sky. "It's freezing out here," Amanda fussed as she pulled her thick, pink wool scarf up over her mouth.

Conrad spotted a man wearing a brown park ranger jacket standing off in the distance. The man waved at Conrad and pointed to a body lying in the snow. "You ladies had better stay here," he said in a concerned voice.

Sarah brushed snow off her white coat and shook her head. "We're big girls, Conrad," she said.

Conrad watched the falling snow land on Sarah's pink ski cap. For a second he forgot all about the dead man and wondered what it would be like to take Sarah's hand and go for a cozy walk in the snow together.

"I'd rather stay right here," Amanda cut in, interrupting his thoughts. "I'm not really keen on seeing a dead body."

Sarah drew in a deep breath of cold air as Amanda hugged her arms together. The winds weren't very strong —at least for the time being. The icy temperature was harsh and yet, as she looked around at the snow-covered lake, the beautiful woods, and the sleeping trees, Sarah saw a beauty that somehow warmed her. Sure, it was cold enough to freeze your thoughts in place, but somehow the cold didn't bother her at the moment. "We'll stay right here then," she agreed. Conrad nodded his head and walked off down the narrow trail that hugged the edge of the lake.

"Maybe a bear got that poor guy," Amanda suggested.

Sarah watched Conrad make his way over to the park ranger, shake hands, and then look down at the body lying on the ground. "Bears are hibernating right now," she pointed out.

"One can only hope a rogue bear woke up," Amanda replied, watching as Conrad bent down. With worried eyes, she watched him methodically examine the body of the dead man. "Please let it be a bear...please, oh please."

Sarah bit down on her lower lip and pushed her gloved hands into the pockets of her coat. It was clear to her from Conrad's manner that the victim had not been attacked by a bear. No, the hands of a human being had taken the life of this park ranger. "The man's death could have to do with Frank Gatti?" she ventured, even though the suggestion seemed very weak in her own mind.

"Let it be a bear...oh, let it be a bear," Amanda begged again.

Sarah saw Conrad stand up. He looked over at her and shook his head. "It wasn't a bear," she told Amanda in a sour voice.

Hearing footsteps behind them, Amanda glanced over her shoulder and saw Andrew approaching. "Ladies," Andrew called and waved a hand at them.

"Send in the cavalry," Amanda sighed with mock misery.

Sarah kept her eyes on Conrad as he began searching the area around the body. Ignoring Andrew's approach, Sarah said to Amanda, "You stay here, okay?" and then walked toward the edge of the lake.

As she approached the crime scene, a tall, stout man with a large belly and round face greeted her. "My name is Sarah Garland," she introduced herself in a professional voice.

"I've heard about you," Park Ranger Dave Dandleton replied, pulling his brown ski cap down over his ears. "Do you want to take a closer look at the body?"

Sarah glanced down. She saw a man in his late forties or early fifties, his brown park ranger's uniform already dusted with snow and his limbs lying peacefully, almost as if he had simply laid down for an ice-bitten, fatal sleep. "Yes," she said and bended down to examine the body in closer detail.

Ten frozen minutes later, Conrad approached her. "Well?" he asked.

Sarah shook her head and stood up, brushing snow off the hem of her dress. "Single needle mark on the left side of the neck. Wallet is missing. No keys. You find anything?"

"No," Conrad said in a disappointed voice. "The body has been out here for a few hours. The wind and snow have covered any tracks left behind."

Dave stared down at the body. "Charlie just transferred up here from Wyoming a few months ago," he said sadly. "I admit that I didn't really take a liking to him, but..." He shook his head in disbelief and looked out across the frozen lake.

"Why didn't you like him?" Sarah asked carefully.

Dave shrugged his shoulders. "No reason," he admitted. "Sometimes you just get a feeling...a vibe...about someone. Charlie came off as cold as a glacier and never attempted to warm up to any of us. Out here, you see, park rangers are a team. Our lives depend on one another."

Sarah nodded her head and looked at Conrad, who was staring down at the body. "Did he ever talk about anyone? Was he married? Did he have any kids?"

Dave shook his head. "I processed his transfer papers," he explained. "I guess Charlie could have lied on his paperwork, but I don't see why he would."

"Why did he transfer to Alaska from Wyoming?" Sarah asked.

"I don't know. He never said. He used to work at Yellowstone," Dave explained, keeping his eyes on the frozen lake. "He spent nearly twenty years there, too." Dave paused and finally turned to focus his eyes on Sarah. "He came highly recommended. After Bert retired, we sure needed a good man with experience. I thought, well, our part of the land was getting a good deal. I was wrong."

"Why?" Conrad asked. "Didn't he do his job?"

"Sure, sure," Dave said and shrugged his shoulders. "Charlie did his job and did it well."

"Then what?" Conrad pressed. "Listen, it's cold out here and I don't feel like waiting around while you drag your feet, okay? A man is dead and I need answers."

Dave looked up, stung but chastened, and he sighed reluctantly. "Charlie preferred to work alone, and even when he had to go out with a team, he still worked alone.

Can you understand that? The man was a loner...he always seemed to have something on his mind and didn't want to be bothered by anyone."

Conrad nodded his head. "I get it," he assured Dave. "So you found the body about three hours ago?"

"Yeah. I put the time down on my log sheet. It's a good walk from the parking area to the lake. I came up from the south trail and started navigating around the lake. I didn't find Charlie until I came around to the north side here."

"And you came out to the lake because...?" Sarah asked.

"After each storm, we check around Diamond Lake for damage...see if a tree has fallen on the lake that could have cracked the ice, check for any fallen signs, make sure the trails are still passable to and from the lake, those kinds of things."

"What was Charlie doing here?" Conrad asked. "Is checking out the area a two-man job?"

Dave shook his head. "Charlie was supposed to have the day off. What he was doing here in his uniform is beyond me."

Sarah studied Dave's face, red from the cold. "Have you seen anyone acting strange lately?" she asked.

Dave shook his head again. "Look around," he said, "this isn't exactly a hot spot. Even in the summer, the most we get up here are fishermen and maybe a hiker or a biker. The truth is, Diamond Lake is just an eight-foot-deep lake sitting out in the middle of nowhere. I know it looks big, but it's shallow with a grassy bottom fed by a natural spring. But the lake is part of the park and, as I said, after each storm, someone has to check this area."

"You didn't spot anyone when you arrived? No vehicles in the parking area?" Conrad asked.

Dave shook his head a third time. "Only Charlie's truck. I wasn't sure what to make of Charlie being out there. The guy did take a liking to this area, so I figured he was out taking an early morning walk or maybe even checking the lake himself. I wasn't really interested in bumping into him. What Charlie was doing on his day off was his business, you know."

Conrad beckoned to Andrew, who was keeping Amanda company. Andrew nodded and hurried over to Conrad. "Coroner is on his way, but it's going to be a bit. It's rough going getting this far out," Andrew said, breathing white trails of condensation from his mouth.

"Got a tarp in your truck?" Conrad asked.

Andrew nodded, then looked down at the body with mournful eyes. "I saw this guy in town a few days back. He was buying some groceries. I tried to strike up a conversation with him because he was wearing his park uniform. I guess he just wasn't in the mood to talk."

Sarah locked eyes with Conrad, who nodded. "Did you see anyone with him?" he asked Andrew.

Andrew shrugged his shoulders. "I guess he could have, but I didn't see anyone. I was in a rush to get home, anyway. I didn't mind too much that he didn't want to talk." He shook his head. "I was hoping...maybe a bear...I knew better, though. I'll go get a tarp from my truck and cover the body."

"I'll walk with you," Dave said, "...if that's okay, Detective?"

"One more question," Sarah said in a patient voice.

"Okay," Dave agreed.

"When you arrived, did you see any prints in the snow, any tracks leading away from the body, anything at all?"

"All I saw," Dave explained, "was Charlie lying on the ground. I sure didn't know what he was doing here, but when I saw him, I thought he had had a heart attack or something. The first thing I did was feel for a pulse and check his breathing. I called the police station and started CPR on him...until I couldn't go any more. But I knew there wasn't anything else I could do for the poor guy...he was dead. I guess I already knew that when I started CPR. His body was already as cold as a glacier."

"Thanks. You did the right thing," said Sarah.

Conrad bent down to examine the body once more.

"Now why would this man transfer all the way up here to Alaska?" he wondered aloud.

"Maybe he was running," Sarah said, squatting down beside him, "but the killer caught up with him. Or maybe he had personal problems back at Yellowstone and wanted a change of scenery? Maybe he didn't get along in his new job and one of the park rangers here killed him?"

"Well, we know he was poisoned," Conrad said, pointing his finger at the needle mark in the man's neck. "He doesn't strike me as the drug addict type.

The autopsy will tell us more." He stood up and looked around. "The killer strikes, covers his tracks, and then fades away into the snow. Sarah, we're going to have to really use our brains on this one."

Sarah stood up. "So far we've dealt with a mentally ill model who builds creepy snowmen and some very dangerous men with deadly intentions. At least on this case, the killer has nothing personal against you or me," she said in a relieved voice.

"I didn't handle the last case very well, did I?" Conrad said miserably. "I let Frank ambush me, and if you hadn't shown up when you did...I would be dead right now, myself. I...really let Sophia get to me. I thought she was dead and couldn't stop blaming myself."

Sarah reached out and touched Conrad's shoulder. "I couldn't stop blaming myself for my divorce. I kept thinking...was it something I did? But I've finally come to realize that sometimes, Conrad, the answers we seek just aren't there."

Conrad nodded. "I know," he agreed and drew in a deep breath. "My mind is straight now," he assured her. "I'm back on level ground and ready to get back to work. A man is dead and we have a killer to find."

"Or killers," Sarah said and immediately wondered why she had said that. But she knew it was likely.

"What do you mean?"

"Look at the position of the body." Sarah pointed down to the snowy ground. "Conrad, this is an open area, plus this man was a park ranger. I doubt anyone was able to overcome him while he was unaware. And just about anyone whose life is in danger is going to put up a fight."

Conrad looked around. Amanda was standing in the distance, cradling her arms together over her chest. Andrew and Dave were walking off toward the south trail. He could see everyone clear as day. "We could have more than one killer, but then again," he pointed out, "maybe the killer was someone he knew? Come on, let's go check out his truck."

Sarah glanced down at the body one last time and walked away with Conrad.

"Well?" Amanda said through frozen lips as the two approached. "What's the bad news?"

"Murder," Conrad said simply, shaking his head as he headed toward the south trail toward the parking area.

Sarah put her arm around Amanda's shoulder. "There was a needle mark on the left side of the neck. Seems like the victim was poisoned," she explained as they walked away from the lake.

"That's creepy," Amanda said, feeling an icy shiver trickle down her spine. Refusing to look back at the lake, she focused her eyes straight on the trail ahead where Conrad was walking several feet ahead of them. "Any ideas?" she asked.

"The victim transferred to Alaska from Yellowstone Park," Sarah said in a thoughtful voice. "Dave, the park ranger you saw walking with Andrew, insists the victim was isolated and impersonal in his thought and actions, a loner. The victim—"

"Please stop saying the word 'victim'!" Amanda begged. "You're really creeping me out."

"Sorry," Sarah said. "The man's name is Charlie, how's that?"

"Better," Amanda replied gratefully, brushing the snow off her bangs and the top of her ski cap as they walked.

"Charlie marked 'single' on his paperwork," Sarah

continued. "No wife and no children. Conrad and I will dig into his past and see who his parents were, if he has any siblings, aunts or uncles, or any close friends that may be of some help to us."

"You should demand payment for your services," Amanda said.

"Fulfilling one's civic duty is reward enough!" Conrad called out over his shoulder.

"You hush up," Amanda fussed at him. "I should make you pay me for my help with more than donuts and hot coffee."

"Civic duty," Conrad called out again. "But I can make sure you're paid with as many donuts as you want."

Sarah grinned. It was good to see Conrad showing a sense of humor, as mild an instance as it might be. "At least this case isn't personal," she told Amanda. "And honestly, I don't mind offering my services for free. Once a cop, always a cop."

Amanda sighed. "I know, I know," she said, keeping her eyes on the snowy trail. But," she added, attempting to sound positive, "it's like you just said, love, at least this case isn't personal...no insane models or crazy mafia nuts."

"That's true," Sarah agreed.

Amanda cleared her throat and spoke in her best mafia

voice: "Forget about it...who is this guy... I'll whack you...now pass the garlic bread or else."

Conrad stopped walking and turned to look at Amanda. "Not bad," he said, impressed.

"Thank you, sir," Amanda replied and brushed past him. "Don't dilly-dally, Detective. We have work to do."

Conrad rolled his eyes. "Yeah, I'm coming." He followed Sarah and Amanda to the parking area. Andrew was leaning over the bed of his truck, fishing out a green tarp. Dave was standing beside him, looking down into a deep gulley that bordered the lot. "I wonder what he's thinking?" Conrad murmured, nodding his head toward Dave.

Sarah removed her arm from around Amanda's shoulder. "Do you think he's hiding something from us?" she asked softly, taking note of the park ranger's brown Subaru parked next to Andrew's truck. Notably, the Subaru appeared to lack sufficient snow accumulation on its hood and roof considering how much snowfall they'd had.

"Could be," Conrad said seriously. He focused on the brown truck parked at the far end of the parking area, which was nothing more than a large, unpaved square with enough parking spaces for eight vehicles. Beyond the east side of it was a deep gully filled with snow, marked off with a metal safety railing. On the west side of the lot was a thick stand of trees. Two wooden signs nailed to two different trees marked the entrances to the south and north hiking trails.

"Come on," he said.

Sarah and Amanda followed Conrad to the brown truck. "The victim's...I mean, Charlie's keys and wallet were missing from his body," Sarah reminded him. "The killer obviously wanted to make the murder appear to be a fatal mugging."

Conrad dipped his head over the bed of the truck. "Clean. Nothing except a spare tire and a jack under the snow in there," he said in a disappointed voice. He went for the driver's side door. To his relief, the door was unlocked. "Let's see what we can find. Sarah, try the other door."

Sarah walked to the passenger's side door and found it unlocked. She pulled it open. "Based on the amount of snow on the hood and roof, this truck's been sitting here for at least three or four hours."

"Yep," Conrad said, studying the interior with skilled eyes.

Sarah carefully opened the glove compartment box and began sifting through its contents. Amanda peered over her shoulder. "Insurance cards...vehicle registration...and a map," she called out to Conrad.

Conrad bent down and studied the underside of the driver's seat. "Clear," he said.

"Let's check behind the seat," Sarah suggested. Conrad located the metal latch, pushed it down, and pulled the seat forward toward the steering wheel. "Clear," Sarah said calmly. "We'll need to check for prints."

"Yep," Conrad said, pushing the seat back into its original position.

Sarah closed the passenger's side door and walked around to Conrad. "Dave's Subaru—"

"Yep," Conrad said again, "it should have more snow on the roof and hood."

"You guys are good," Amanda whispered.

"Training," Sarah explained, "and years of trial and error, ups and downs, good and bad."

Conrad casually walked over to the brown Subaru and slid his hand under the snow covering the hood. "Cold," he told Sarah and Amanda. He spotted Dave standing a little ways off, regarding him with worried eyes. "Come on," said Conrad to the two women.

Conrad walked over to where Dave and Andrew stood, where Andrew was shaking snow off the green tarp in his hands. "Why did you lie?" Conrad asked Dave without preamble.

Andrew's head shot up and he stopped shaking the snow off the tarp. "Is there a problem?" he asked.

"Ask him," Conrad said, nodding his head at Dave, who had a look of panic in his eyes. "You haven't been here very long, have you, Dave? I'd say your story is missing some time."

Dave nervously looked back at his Subaru. He could see now that the lack of snow on the car marked him as guilty. "I..." He began to speak, but hesitated.

"Talk to me or go to jail," Conrad snapped.

Dave swallowed nervously. "I..." he began again, and then his shoulders sagged in defeat. "Okay, okay," he admitted, "I didn't arrive at the lake at the time I logged in on my arrival sheet. I...made a side stop."

"Where?" Conrad demanded.

"Betty Capple's house," Dave admitted in a low, embarrassed voice. "Betty and I are seeing each other, okay? I mean, what's the big deal, anyway? Was there any rush to get out to the lake and pick up a fallen sign or lug a fallen tree off the ice? Who cares if I stop at Betty's house for a cup of coffee and a slice of apple pie?"

Conrad looked at Sarah and saw her reading Dave's eyes. He could tell by the expression on her face that Dave was telling the truth. "Okay, good enough," he said.

"Is it?" Dave asked, the misery plain in his voice. "I mean, what if I had arrived on time? Maybe...just maybe I might have been able to help Charlie. But no," he said, "I had to stop for coffee and pie. How was I supposed to know Charlie was out there, huh? Maybe he wasn't anybody's best friend, but that don't make a difference when you're dying. Nobody should die out in the cold like that." Tears began dripping from his eyes. "I swear if I had known...I would have...I'm sorry I lied, okay?"

"I understand," Conrad said and patted Dave on the shoulder. "How were you supposed to know?"

A thought suddenly struck Sarah. "May I ask you a question?"

"Sure, go ahead." Dave wiped his tears away.

"Would Charlie have known you were going to make a check of this area?"

"We have a duty roster back at headquarters," Dave explained. "There's only four of us...me, Shelia, Matt and...well, Charlie. A ranger has to be on duty twenty-four seven. I make out the duty roster and the schedule and post them a week in advance." His voice quavered as he said this, as if he was realizing for the first time that Charlie would never be on the roster again. Anyway..." Dave shielded his eyes from the sun with one hand, clearing his throat to steady himself again. "Anyway, everyone knows the ranger on morning duty is responsible for checking the green areas after any storm."

"Green areas?"

"For us park rangers, that means lakes, picnic areas, playgrounds, camping areas, rental cabins, RV areas. Anything that's not a forest, basically. It's a shame Diamond Lake is so remote that all we have to offer is a few lakeside areas, some hiking trails and a camping area that is seldom used. Denali National Park is the state's hot spot. Our little park, even though it's beautiful, just doesn't bring in many people."

"Charlie would have known you were assigned to check the lake this morning, then," Sarah concluded.

"Yeah, I guess so." Dave shook his head regretfully. "Do you think maybe...Charlie came here because he needed my help?"

Conrad looked toward the entrance to the south trail. "Who knows?" he said. "But it does seem interesting that the deceased showed up in an area where he knew a fellow co-worker would be arriving sooner or later."

Sarah bit down on her lower lip. "Charlie was wearing his ranger uniform...maybe he didn't want the killer—or killers—to think he had the day off?"

"Possible," Conrad agreed.

"Killers?" Dave asked, taken aback.

Conrad shook his head. "We'll talk more down at the

station. I'm going to need you to come down and make a statement, okay?"

"I..." Dave hesitated, then nodded. "I guess I can call Shelia in early."

Andrew looked at the tarp he was still holding. "Well, I'd better go cover the body. You coming with me, Detective?"

"Yeah," Conrad answered. "Sarah, Amanda, you girls take Andrew's truck and drive back into town. Andrew can ride back with me."

"I'll start seeing what I can dig up," Sarah promised. She looked at Dave. "I'm going to need Charlie's full name and Social Security number."

"Of course," Dave agreed. "I'll make a pit stop at headquarters and get his personnel file for you."

Conrad nodded. "You can use the computer in my office," he told Sarah and then walked off through the snowy parking area with Andrew.

"Ms. Garland?" Dave asked as they watched Conrad and Andrew walk toward the north trail.

"Yes?"

"Me, Shelia and Matt weren't fond of Charlie," he said, "but he was still one of us. Is it possible that whoever killed Charlie might come after other park rangers?"

Sarah hadn't considered that possibility yet. She looked into Dave's worried eyes. "I don't know," she answered honestly.

Dave shoved his hands into the pockets of his coat and looked down into the gulley again. He didn't say another word, and they left him alone with his thoughts in the quiet, gray light. Amanda gave Sarah a worried look and walked to the passenger side of Andrew's truck, opened the door, and climbed into the cabin. Sarah watched Conrad and Andrew disappear down the north trail into the snowy unknown.

CHAPTER TWO

Sarah leaned back in Conrad's office chair and rubbed her neck with tired hands. "Charlie Edward Raymond was a fifty-one-year-old man who spent his entire life in Wyoming. He graduated from high school in a small Wyoming town, went to college in Wyoming, worked a series of uninteresting jobs, and began working for the National Park Service at the age of twenty-eight."

Amanda sat across the desk from Sarah, eating the cheeseburger she had bought from the local diner. "Any family?"

"No," Sarah said, "and that's what's strange. Charlie Raymond seems to have been a confirmed bachelor. He was an only child and his mother died when he was forty and his dad died when he was forty-three." She continued to rub her neck. "He does have an aunt in Georgia who is eighty-four years old."

Amanda was still working on her cheeseburger. "Any reason why he left his beloved Wyoming?"

Sarah began rubbing her eyes. "Not a clue...yet."

"You need to eat. Your food is getting cold."

"Huh? Oh, sure." Sarah stopped rubbing her eyes. Looking down at her white carryout container, a cheeseburger, french fries, and a slice of pecan pie stared up at her. "Are you trying to get me fat?" she joked.

"I'm depressed, okay?" Amanda replied, upset and apologetic. "My Jack isn't coming home anytime soon. He's been delayed in London."

"When did this happen?" Sarah asked in a sympathetic tone, forgetting about the food again.

"An hour ago. I called Jack when I walked down to the diner," Amanda explained, finishing off her cheeseburger. "He said he was going to call me tonight and tell me."

"Is he being delayed because of his dad?"

Amanda nodded her head. "Who else?" she said and picked up a few french fries. "You know, there are times when I could just punch that smelly old goat of a man right in the nose."

"I'm sorry," Sarah said, laughing. "You still have me, though."

"And frozen feet, frostbite, double pneumonia, nightmares and a whole bunch of mean people who now know who I am and what I look like," Amanda added. "I really don't think I'll tell Jack about that sour old Gatti bloke."

"Sorry about that," Sarah said remorsefully. "I guess being my friend is kinda hazardous, huh?"

Amanda stared at Sarah for a moment and then offered her friend a loving smile. "You can pay my medical bills when I end up in the hospital with pneumonia."

"Deal," Sarah promised and picked up her cheeseburger. "So, any thoughts on the case?" she asked.

Amanda munched on her french fries. "I keep thinking about what Dave said. What if there is someone out there...some crazy felon who is targeting park rangers?"

Sarah took a bite of the cheeseburger. "So good," she said. "I guess I'm hungrier than I thought."

"Then eat, love. You need your energy."

"We actually have two mysteries to solve," Sarah mused. "Is someone targeting park rangers? And why did Charlie Raymond move to Alaska? The two questions might be connected, they might not. I still think it's possible he was an isolated target. But," Sarah added, thinking back on her years of experience, "there is always the unknown variable that lingers in the darkness."

"So you think Mr. Raymond was running from someone who caught up to him?" Amanda asked.

Sarah nodded. "For now," she admitted. "I also think that there might be more than one person involved in the murder, too."

"I was afraid of that," Amanda said in a worried voice. "But, for now, let's just pretend that the killer...or killers...is targeting park rangers. Let me explain."

"Please," Sarah said amiably, taking another bite of her cheeseburger.

Amanda stood up. "Suppose the killer or killers originally only wanted Mr. Raymond dead, right?"

"Okay."

"But now the killer...or killers," Amanda said, slowly pacing around Conrad's office, "may go after the other park rangers Mr. Raymond worked with because he...she...or they...fear Mr. Raymond might have talked to the other park rangers."

"Not bad," Sarah complimented her friend.

"I watched an old rerun of 'Murder, She Wrote' last night," Amanda confessed. "Jessica was trying to prove who killed someone on a bus on a very rainy, stormy night," she finished in her best spooky Scotland Yard voice.

"Be that as it may, you make a vital point," Sarah said gratefully. "Whoever killed Charlie Raymond, whether it be one person or two, might go after the other park rangers to silence them."

"So that means we need to warn them, right?"

"We'd better wait and see what Conrad thinks. I don't have the authority to do that," Sarah explained. "If anyone caught me using Conrad's computer, he could be in a lot of trouble. But this is a small town and Andrew is a good man who looks the other way when needed."

"You could always come out of retirement," Amanda suggested.

"Oh no," Sarah said, shaking her head, "this town only has enough room for one detective. We're offering a helping hand and nothing more. I'm perfectly content with my coffee shop and writing my books. And speaking of books, I'm falling way behind. My publisher isn't going to be happy."

"You tell your publisher that murder is serious," Amanda said playfully, "and that your talents are needed away from the keyboard."

"Easier said than done," Sarah grimaced. She put down her cheeseburger and picked up a cup full of hot coffee.

"Conrad is going to have to question the people Charlie Raymond worked with at Yellowstone," she said, trying to forget the reminder of her missed writing deadlines.

"Good idea," Amanda said as she sat back down. Drawing in a deep breath, she quickly grabbed a slice of pecan pie out of the carryout container. "I blame you for the future fat rolls, Jack," she said and took a bite of the pie.

Sarah laughed. "I'm sure Jack will love your future fat rolls."

Amanda shrugged her shoulders. "If he doesn't then I'll hide his custard tarts from him. Custard tarts are Jack's one weakness."

Sarah leaned back in Conrad's chair. "My husband and I...we used to know each other's weaknesses. Mine was always mint chocolate chip cookies."

Amanda could hear the sorrow in Sarah's voice behind the reminiscence. "It's so sad that the divorce rate is up. Not only in America but everywhere. People can't commit to love anymore. I was reading an article a few weeks ago by a man named Oliver Halcomb who has been married for over fifty years. And do you know what this man wrote about?"

"The secret to love?" Sarah took a wild guess.

"Nope," Amanda said. She put down her pecan pie. "Mr.

Halcomb wrote that marriage is from God and unless people commit to God, they can't have a successful marriage. Now, as a Christian, I agree with him. Every day Jack and I pray together and manage to read our Bibles as a couple."

"My ex-husband and I never read our Bibles together," Sarah admitted. "He was more of an agnostic. He never minded when I went to church, but he did always seem to dodge the question of God when I brought it up...so I stopped."

"People are weak," Amanda stated not unkindly. "They want love and romance and those warm fuzzy feelings. But when they find out marriage takes work, they run for the nearest divorce lawyer and then begin the search for love and romance and those warm fuzzy feelings all over again, hoping to land the right fish, only to come up empty-handed, over and over again."

"Love does take...commitment," Sarah agreed.

"It sure does," Amanda said emphatically. "When I kiss my husband, I don't feel warm and fuzzy all over...not the way I did when we first met. Instead, I feel security and comfort. I feel that I'm home. Jack and I sure go around the table sometimes, but at the end of the day, we always make up. I realize that he's human and he realizes that I'm human. I accept that he has bad breath when he wakes up and he accepts that I have some very wacky hair days." Amanda took a breath and looked gently into Sarah's eyes. "What I'm trying to say is that...well, you got caught in a bad deal, love. You married a bad fish who wasn't willing to work at his marriage."

"He just stopped loving me," Sarah said, feeling tears sting her eyes. "My ex-husband just stopped loving me."

"You can fall in love—when it's real love—but you can't fall out of love if the love was real."

Sarah, comforted, gazed at her friend in admiration. "You're a very blessed woman to have a husband like Jack."

"Yeah, I guess I am," Amanda smiled. "But love, I'm not going to let you spend the rest of your life alone. Somewhere out there, your Jack is waiting...your real Jack."

Before Sarah could answer, the door to the office opened and Conrad stepped in, his coat stiff and frosted with gray. "Wind really started picking up at the lake," he said in a voice that told Sarah and Amanda that he was grateful to be back inside a warm building. "Find out anything yet?"

Sarah began to get up from his chair but Conrad gestured for her to remain seated and sat down next to Amanda instead. "Well," Sarah said, pushing the thought of her ex-husband out of her mind, "I confirmed that Charlie Raymond had no wife or children. Both of his parents are dead. The only living relative seems to be an aunt who is living in an assisted living center in Georgia."

"Pecan pie?" Amanda asked Conrad, offering him her half-eaten pie.

"No thanks," Conrad said. Instead, he reached forward and plucked Sarah's coffee off of the desk. "I need coffee."

Sarah smiled, glad to know it was still hot enough to warm his stiff hands. "Did you discover anything else at the lake before the coroner arrived?" Sarah asked.

"Yes and no," he replied. "After Andrew covered the body with the tarp, we decided to explore the surrounding woods some. We spent about forty minutes out there." Conrad took a big gulp of coffee. "Andrew found a single piece of gray thread stuck to a low-hanging tree limb."

"How far back into the woods were you when Andrew found the thread?" Sarah asked.

"Maybe a quarter of a mile?" Conrad took a guess. "The woods just keep running north. Andrew didn't want to go too far in. To be honest, I didn't either. It's too easy to get turned around and lose your way."

Sarah nodded her head. "It's possible the piece of thread belonged to the killer."

Conrad finished off Sarah's coffee in another gulp and set

the cup down on his desk. "No boot prints, no snowmobile tracks, nothing," he said. "I'm going to question the other park rangers and then make a few calls to Yellowstone. Maybe someone there can help us out."

"Dave wrote out his statement. He wanted to leave, but I asked that he wait for you. Did you see him out in the front lobby?"

Conrad nodded. "I told him to leave and send his co-workers down to the station for questioning."

"I think I'll stick around myself," Sarah said, then nodded her head at Amanda. "Amanda made a good point a few minutes ago, Conrad. She suggested that the killer...or killers...might try to go after the three remaining park rangers."

Amanda turned in her chair to face Conrad. "I was thinking that maybe the killers...he...she...they...whoever...might think Mr. Raymond talked to the other park rangers, you know. I mean, the man was obviously killed for some reason or another, and the killer, or whoever, might think the other park rangers know that reason."

"Amanda watched a rerun of 'Murder, She Wrote' last night," Sarah smiled.

Conrad didn't smile. The suggestion held strong credibility. "Good thinking, Amanda. Thanks a lot," he said thoughtfully and reached for his phone. "Andrew, I want Dave, Shelia, and Matt all back at the station. Their lives could be in danger. Yes, now." He put down the receiver. "One of the park rangers could be the killer, but then again, maybe not. But we have to assume they're innocent until proven otherwise."

"Why do you think one of the park rangers could be the killer?" Amanda asked.

"Charlie was a loner. So who else knew he liked the area around the lake except for his fellow park rangers?" Conrad pointed out. "Now, there is a chance he knew the killer and made arrangements to meet at the lake, too. So, until we begin narrowing down the possibilities, we have to make broad assumptions and mark everyone as a suspect."

"Except Dave," Sarah pointed out.

Conrad hesitated and then nodded. "I don't think Dave killed Charlie Raymond," he confessed. "But we still have to treat him as if he did for now."

Sarah slowly stood up. "I'll let you call Yellowstone," she said. "Amanda and I will be at my coffee shop. You can have the rest of my food if you're hungry."

"Starving," Conrad admitted gratefully. "But listen, you two stick around. I want you here when our three park ranger friends arrive."

"My coffee shop is just a few blocks away," Sarah

protested. "Just ring me when they arrive and we'll come running."

"Okay," Conrad agreed. He was looking at Sarah's takeout container of food. "And bring some more coffee when you come back."

"You got it," Sarah promised. She walked to the wooden coat rack next to the office door and grabbed her coat. "Conrad, my gut is telling me more than one person is involved in this killing."

"Why?"

"Yeah, why?" Amanda echoed, taking her own coat off the coat rack.

"Charlie's body position was too perfect," Sarah explained with the voice of an expert. "I could tell that Dave disturbed the body when he was performing CPR. However, even with that bit of disturbance, the body was still in a far too perfect position. I didn't see any signs of a struggle, any bruises, bleeding, or scratches on the body or any tears in the uniform." Sarah put on her coat. "At the location where the body was found, it would have been nearly impossible to ambush the victim. Either Charlie Raymond knew his attackers, or he was shot in the neck from a distance with the poison that probably killed him."

"The distance from the edge of the woods to the lake makes that type of shot nearly impossible," Conrad pointed out. "Only an expert could have carried out a shot from that distance."

"I agree," Sarah said as she opened the office door. "Which leads us back to door number one: Charlie Raymond knew his attackers."

"I'd better get on the phone with the people at Yellowstone," Conrad said and stood up.

"We'll be at my coffee shop," Sarah promised. "Ready, Amanda?"

"Ready, partner," Amanda said and pulled on her ski hat. "Conrad, I'll bring back some cinnamon buns along with the coffee. Something tells me we have a very long night ahead of us."

"Thanks," Conrad said and hurried behind his desk. Without saying another word, he snatched up his phone and got to work. Sarah tilted her head toward the hallway. Amanda put her finger to her lip and quietly followed Sarah out of the office. Outside, a heavy snow began to fall.

CHAPTER THREE

"The weatherman didn't predict any snow for today," Amanda said, shivering. Walking beside Sarah down a sidewalk covered with rock salt, she felt like a woman out of a mystery novel, walking beside a tough cop and searching the streets of some dangerous metropolis for criminals.

Sarah glanced up into the low, dark, cold gray sky. "Well, it's snowing now," she said and stopped walking.

"What?" Amanda asked. "Why did you stop walking?"

Sarah pointed at the display window of a cozy bakery. The window was filled with delicious cakes, cookies, donuts, muffins, and pies. "This is what life should be," she told Amanda. "Life should be this display window...warm, cozy, inviting...safe. But instead, life is full of murder, danger, crime, hate...why? Why do people insist on acting like animals instead of human beings? In all my years in law enforcement, I could never understand why."

Amanda examined the display. She settled her gaze on a mouthwatering coconut cake with miniature ice skater figurines on top of it. "It's been a while since Jack and I have been ice skating," she said sadly. "Sometimes we get so caught up in everyday living that we forget the important stuff. I guess that's the way it is for some people...the bad ones, I mean. They just forget that God created us with a heart and depend on the darkness inside of them instead."

"How much darkness has to be in a person to allow them to take another life?"

"Not how much darkness is in them," Amanda corrected Sarah. "The question is: How dark has that person allowed him or herself to become? How dark peoples' hearts can become over the years is a very scary thing. Crime doesn't stop at the American shoreline, love. Back in London, you would be amazed at the rate of murder. Drugs...alcohol...hate...violence...there always seems to be a trigger for people to kill themselves with."

"A few years back, in Los Angeles," Sarah said, gazing at a cozy box of donuts covered with sprinkles, "I was assigned to a homicide case that involved a married couple. The husband had killed his wife and claimed that a home invader had carried out the gruesome attack. He carried out so many elaborate deceptions to make his home look as if it had been broken into. The only problem was he tried too hard and became entangled in his own lies."

"How horrible," Amanda said. "I hope they locked the creep up and threw away the keys."

Sarah kept staring at the donuts. "He was a rich guy with enough money to hire the best defense team money could find. In the end, the guy claimed that his wife tried to kill him and he fought back in self-defense but then panicked. Needless to say, he was acquitted."

"You're kidding me," Amanda exclaimed, shocked.

"A jury of his peers found him not guilty," Sarah said in a disgusted voice. "That's when I knew that my time as a homicide detective was really coming to an end. I had done my job, captured a killer, and brought peace to a suffering family, only to have a bunch of bleeding-hearts throw justice back in my face."

"My goodness," Amanda said in disbelief.

"Money talks." Sarah looked up into the snowy sky. "I know it's very cold here and the snow can sometimes be a bit too much, but it's quiet, small, and cozy. The last thing I would have ever expected was all this trouble in such a small town."

Amanda glanced up at the falling snow. "I fuss about the

snow, but honestly, love, I adore it. I adore every single snowflake. The snow makes life seem clean and pure to me. But," she added, "if we don't get out of this cold right now, you and I are going to turn into icebergs."

The thought of a hot cup of coffee pulled Sarah away from the display window. She began carefully walking down the sidewalk, taking care not to slip on the icy, compacted snow. "Hey," she said suddenly, "look at that poor little thing over there."

"Oh my," Amanda said, following Sarah's eyes and spotting a stray kitten curled up against the doorstep of a hardware store. "The poor dear."

Sarah approached the kitten. It began crying. "It's okay," she said in a soothing voice. She carefully picked the kitten up and placed it inside her coat. "You're freezing."

"I think the little bloke is an orange tabby," Amanda observed.

"Let's hurry and get it inside. I'll give it a warm bowl of milk at the coffee shop."

Sarah and Amanda hurried to the closed coffee shop. Once inside, they hung up their coats and ventured into the kitchen. "I'll take the wee thing," Amanda offered.

Sarah handed Amanda the kitten and quickly walked to the refrigerator to retrieve a carton of milk. "Poor thing must be starving," she said.

"No collar or tag," Amanda said, petting the kitten's neck. The kitten, realizing it was safe and warm, began purring in Amanda's hands. "Well, what do you know, the little bum likes me."

Sarah opened the carton and poured some milk into a small silver pot sitting on the stove. "Hold on, little guy," she said. "Dinner is about to be served, and—" Sarah stopped talking as a movement from her office caught her eye. In one quick flash, she bent down, grabbed the gun from the holster attached to her right ankle, and yelled: "You, in my office, come out with your hands up, now!"

Amanda ran behind Sarah, cradling the kitten in her arms. "Yeah...we've got you surrounded," she called out with false bravado.

The first thing Sarah saw emerge from her office was the silver tip of a cane. A distinguished-looking older man followed. "No need for violence, my dear." He spoke in a calm, precise tone.

Despite his intelligent tone, Sarah stared at him in shock. She could barely believe her eyes. How in the world had this man broken into her coffee shop—and *why* would he break into her coffee shop? "Who are you?" she demanded, keeping her gun at the ready.

The man lifted his left hand and brushed at the expensive gray suit he was wearing. "My name is Bradley

Preston," he answered in a relaxed voice that betrayed no concern for the gun still pointed at him.

Amanda stared at the man and absorbed his features. Neatly combed thin gray hair, neatly trimmed thin gray mustache, neatly alert gray eyes, neatly pressed gray suit, neatly shined gray shoes, neatly polished gray cane with a silver tip...he was nearly all gray. "You're British," she said.

"Indeed," Bradley replied. Raising his cane, he pointed at the cat Amanda held in her arms. "Please keep that feline far from me. I have certain allergies that do not agree with cats."

"Who are you?" Sarah repeated, keeping her voice firm. "I want answers, Mr. Preston."

"I've come for a killer," Bradley answered, keeping his tone even. He sounded almost bored. "Or, should I say killers?"

"You know who murdered Charlie Raymond?" Sarah asked.

"Indeed," Bradley said, finally locking eyes with Sarah. "However, I am not here to offer assistance to you women. My objective today in making this personal visit is to request that you stand down, Ms. Garland. I will track down the killers, relieve you of their threat and vanish into the wind."

"Oh my," Amanda said in alarm.

"What?" Sarah asked. "Amanda, speak to me."

"This man...I believe he's British intelligence. You know, MI-6 Los Angeles, do as this man asks, please," Amanda explained in a frightened voice.

Bradley shifted his glance to Amanda. "You are a very smart woman. I'm sure Jack would be well pleased to hear you make such a wise suggestion to Detective Garland."

"Get your hands up in the air," Sarah ordered Bradley. "I don't care who you are or how you know Jack. A murder has taken place and you have just admitted that you know the killers. I'm placing you under arrest unless you can prove your identity."

"My dear, you are retired, are you not?" Bradley asked. "Under whose authority are you detaining me?"

"I'm making a citizen's arrest," Sarah answered bravely.

"Los Angeles," Amanda whispered, scared out of her wits, "you don't know who this man is. Please, do as he asks."

"A man has been murdered," Sarah answered in an even tone. "I have a duty."

"Oh dear," Amanda said. "We're dead...so very dead. Goodbye Jack..."

Bradley shook his head at Amanda. "My dear girl," he said drily, "I have no intention of harming anyone, if you cooperate. My only objective is to catch my quarry and then leave." Bradley looked at Sarah again. "Detective Garland, I certainly can't force you to stand down, but I will warn you that if you get in my way, I may be forced to take extreme measures to ensure my objective is carried out successfully."

Sarah slowly lowered her gun. "Mr. Bradley," she said evenly, "you know that I will not be able to stand down. The wisest path for us to take is to work as a team."

"I'm afraid that will not be possible. The people I am after are very vicious, rabid animals that must be hunted as such. I have no need for a part-time...sleuth. I must work alone in catching them."

"You mean killing them," Sarah said.

"Oh no," Bradley assured her, "my objective is to simply catch these animals. If in the future they are put down, then that will be the decision of someone who has more authority than I."

Sarah wasn't sure how to proceed. "Mr. Raymond knew something he shouldn't have, is that it?" she asked, quickly fishing for whatever scraps of information she might be able to obtain. "Mr. Raymond acquired very important data that should not have come into his hands?"

Bradley sighed. "Detective Garland, I made my objective clear. Please, dear, agree to my terms. If you fail to listen to me, however, perhaps I will be forced to end Detective Spencer's career earlier than he anticipates."

"Hands up," Sarah ordered in response, raising her gun again. "I'm placing you under citizen's arrest."

Bradley swiveled his eyes to Amanda. "Speak sense to this woman," he commanded her in a cold voice that clearly told Amanda he was finished with polite talk.

Amanda placed the kitten down on the kitchen counter and slowly reached out to touch the gun in Sarah's hands. "He'll kill all of us, Sarah. Please listen to me. As your friend, I'm begging you to put your gun down. This man is MI-6. These people are worse than your CIA. They have weapons that you Yanks can only dream of having."

Sarah thought back to the needle hole on the side of Charlie Raymond's neck. "Who killed Charlie Raymond?" she demanded, her gun still firmly pointed at Bradley.

"Los Angeles, please," Amanda begged, and then with one strong, swift motion she pushed the gun in Sarah's hand down. "Listen to me, this man will kill us," she nearly yelled, hysterical to get her point across.

Sarah looked into Amanda's terrified eyes. "Stand down," Bradley warned as he began walking toward the back door. "Detective Garland, I appreciate your dedication to duty, but certain matters must be handled at a higher pay grade than 'volunteer town detective'."

"I'm not standing down," Sarah warned. "You can insult me, but I won't back down. I'm going to fight you. Detective Spencer will fight you. We won't submit to your threats."

Bradley stopped at the door and threw a deadly look at Sarah. "Then be prepared to die."

"Get out of my kitchen," Sarah retorted, "before I shoot you myself."

Bradley opened the door and left without saying another word. "Oh love," Amanda said in an incredulous voice, "you just signed our death certificates."

Sarah stared at the back door. "Here in America, June Bug, we don't back down. If that man wanted us dead, we would be dead. He could have killed us when we were out at the lake. He came here to make a threat that he has no intention of carrying out."

"How do you know that?" Amanda asked in a scared voice. She snatched the kitten up into her arms again. "Los Angeles, you Yanks have a thing or two to learn about the British."

"How did you know he was British intelligence?" Sarah asked as she cautiously inched her way toward the back door.

"His appearance," Amanda confessed. "I can't explain it, love...his appearance told me what I needed to know."

"He must have someone waiting for him close by, because he walked outside without a coat," Sarah said. She eased open the back door and poked her head out into the snowy, dirty alley. Bradley was nowhere to be seen, but she did spot his footprints heading out of the alley. Without wasting another second, she dashed out of the kitchen and ran in the direction of the prints. When she reached the end of the alley, she turned just in time to see a gray SUV driving away. Shielding her eyes from the snow, Sarah desperately tried to make out the license plate. "Temporary tag," she said out loud in disappointment.

"You're going to get us killed," Amanda said, running up behind her. "And of course, I'm crazy enough to chase after you."

Sarah watched the gray SUV turn right on a side street and vanish around the corner. "Come on," she said and turned to run back to her coffee shop.

"We're dead," Amanda moaned, following Sarah.

Sarah burst into the kitchen and rushed to her office. Plopping down in the office chair, she bent down to replace the gun in her ankle holster and then called Conrad. "We had a visitor," she said grimly, still breathing hard.

Amanda closed and locked the back door to the alley, and then walked into Sarah's office. Her face was twisted in fear. "British intelligence," she muttered miserably, "of all the places in the world..."

"Who?" Conrad asked, hearing the alarm in Sarah's voice.

"A Mr. Bradley Preston...British intelligence," Sarah explained.

"MI-6?" Conrad exclaimed. She heard the squeak of his office chair as he sat bolt upright in alarm.

"Seems to be," Sarah said. "I saw him leave in a gray SUV with temporary tags. He ordered me to stand down from this case or else he would take drastic action, beginning with you."

"MI-6... Are you sure, Sarah?" he asked.

"Amanda is sure."

"And of course my crazy friend threatens the deadly bloke," Amanda yelled toward the phone.

"Go get the kitten some milk, please," Sarah begged Amanda.

"'Go get the kitten some milk'," Amanda nearly laughed to herself. "We're dead and she wants me to fetch warm milk." Amanda looked down at the kitten in her arms.

"Well, why not? No sense in you being hungry. Come on, little guy."

Conrad, his voice still full of concern, said, "Sarah, are you absolutely sure your visitor was MI-6?"

"When Amanda said Mr. Bradley was British intelligence, the man didn't actually confirm her words, but he sure didn't deny the claim, either." Sarah attempted to gather her thoughts. "Conrad, despite his words, I don't think Mr. Bradley has any intention of harming us. If this man is who Amanda says he is, then he could have easily killed us at the lake."

"How do you know he was at the lake?" Conrad asked, confused.

"That piece of gray thread Andrew found," Sarah explained. "This man was wearing a gray suit. It's likely he was wearing a gray coat, as well."

"That's a stretch."

"Then how else do you explain this man showing up at my coffee shop if he didn't see us at the lake?" Sarah nearly yelled into the phone. "Oh, I'm sorry. I didn't mean to—"

"It's okay," Conrad assured her. "And you're right."

Sarah closed her eyes. "Mr. Bradley did confirm my theory that more than one person was involved in the killing of Charlie Raymond."

"He did?"

"Yes." Sarah pictured the landscape of Diamond Lake in her mind. She concentrated on the snowy woods surrounding the lake. "Conrad," she said, "Mr. Bradley isn't alone here. We know he has a driver. He has too many angles to cover on this job to go after the killers alone. If he is British intelligence—"

"The old bloke is MI-6, Los Angeles!" Amanda yelled from the kitchen.

Sarah sighed. "If Mr. Bradley is MI-6, then we're part of something that's very dangerous," she said. "Conrad, you and I both know British intelligence wouldn't make an appearance on American soil unless a serious threat was at hand."

"I'm very familiar with MI-6," Conrad informed Sarah. "When I worked in New York I had a friend who used to work for British intelligence, okay? Let me just tell you that he vanished into thin air. When I tried to open a case on his disappearance, the mayor of New York personally threatened my job and future if I didn't throw the case into the cold files."

"So what do we do, Conrad? Do we throw Mr. Raymond's murder into the cold files and look the other way?"

"I made contact with a Mr. Pence at Yellowstone. He was on his way to a meeting and told me that he would give me a call back within the next hour. Let me see what this guy has to say."

"Who is this Mr. Pence?" Sarah asked.

"Charlie Raymond's former boss," Conrad answered. "Hey, you and Amanda had better get back to my office, okay? From now on we stay by each other's side day and night."

"I don't like being scared and I don't like being threatened," Sarah said, clearing her throat. "I've tangled with some of the worst people mankind has to offer, Conrad. But I'm not going to back down and run scared from a man who hides behind his government agency to bully people."

Conrad was quiet for a moment on his end of the phone before he spoke again. "Sarah, the CIA works closely with the MI-6. If we make one wrong move, it's over for us. Our best shot is to gather up as much information as we can, because whatever information we gather could save our lives."

"You mean to use our information as a bulletproof vest," Sarah inferred.

"Yes," Conrad said. "Listen, you and Amanda get back to my office on the double."

"We're on our way," Sarah promised. She hung up the

phone and walked out of her office into the kitchen. "Conrad wants us back at his office ASAP."

"Let the little kitten eat first," Amanda said, pouring warm milk into a green bowl she had placed on the floor. The kitten ran to the bowl and began hungrily licking up the milk. "Los Angeles...I have Jack to think about. That MI-6 bloke mentioned my husband's name. I know you have your duty, but...I have mine too. I think I'm going to go home and let you run solo this time, okay?" she said in a careful voice. "You know I love you, but...I can't let anything happen to my Jack."

Sarah stared into Amanda's worried eyes. She saw tears appear. "Oh, sweetheart," she said, pulling Amanda into her arms. "I understand. I'll have Andrew drive you home."

Amanda wiped at her tears. "I have my truck parked outside, remember? Listen, Los Angeles, I can't lose my husband over a dead man that I don't even know. Whatever is happening is none of my concern. I was crazy to get involved to begin with."

"You saved my life because you had the courage to care and become involved," Sarah pointed out.

"My courage...is gone," Amanda said, tears welling up again. Leaning up, she looked deep into Sarah's eyes. "Come home with me. We'll make tea and watch a silly romantic comedy and cry our eyes out. Afterward, we'll do each other's nails and fuss about getting old."

Sarah reached out her right hand and wiped Amanda's tears away. "I'm a cop. Once a cop, always a cop. A man was murdered on American soil and I have a job to do. Conrad has a job to do. The police in this town have a job to do."

"I was afraid you would say that," Amanda said, sniffling. "I'd better...go get my coat."

Sarah's heart broke as she watched Amanda leave the kitchen. "Goodbye, partner," she said, fighting back her own tears. Then she followed her friend to the door.

Outside, Amanda slowly walked to her truck, which she had parked in front of the coffee shop. The snow was falling heavier and the winds were picking up. "Another storm is coming," she told Sarah.

"You'd better take this little guy, then," Sarah said and handed Amanda the kitten. "I'll call you tonight, okay? Please, keep your doors locked and don't open up for anyone."

"Trust me," Amanda promised as she pulled open the driver's side door, "I won't. After what we've been through, the only person I'm opening my front door for is Jack."

Sarah watched Amanda place the kitten gently inside the cab of the truck. "I...I'll miss you."

"This isn't goodbye, silly," Amanda said, forcing a smile to her lips. "We're still best friends. I'll still come over to your cabin for some good chats and you'll still come over to my flat for some tea. We'll still go shopping together and grow old together, fussing about our wrinkles."

"I know," Sarah said and hugged Amanda. "It just feels that we're somehow...being separated."

"We're not," Amanda promised, hugging Sarah back. "Now listen to me," she said. "I'm going to drive home, make some coffee, bake some cookies, and call my bloody husband and fuss at him until his ears fall off. Afterward I'll make myself a hot bath, soak until I turn into a prune, and then cuddle up with a silly romantic comedy and cry my eyes out."

"Sounds fun," Sarah smiled. She helped Amanda up into the cab of her truck. "I'll call you," she promised as a strong gust of wind howled down the street in an eerie, lonely voice.

"The wind can sound so creepy at times," Amanda said, looking up the deserted street.

"I know," Sarah agreed. She closed the car door for her friend. Backing up onto the sidewalk, she waved at Amanda. Amanda waved back, brought her truck to life, let it warm up a bit, backed up into the street, and drove away.

"Be safe," Amanda pleaded, glancing at her friend's retreating figure in the rearview mirror. She spotted Conrad walking down the street toward the coffee shop and waved at him as she drove past, too.

Confused, Conrad waved back, then noticed Sarah and hurried up to her. "Where is she going?" he asked.

"Home," Sarah said sadly. "Mr. Bradley threatened her husband. I don't believe he'd follow through, but Amanda was spooked by it. It's different for her, Conrad. I can't blame her."

Conrad shoved his bare hands down into the pockets of his black coat. He watched Amanda's truck as it disappeared in the distance. "Weather report said another storm is pushing in from the west. So much for the clear skies that were predicted."

"The weather can be very unpredictable." Sarah sighed as Amanda's truck vanished from sight. "So, what are you doing here?"

"Personal escort," Conrad explained. "I hurried down here as fast as I could after we hung up. I didn't want you ladies walking back to the police station alone."

"That's very nice of you," Sarah said, grateful for Conrad's unexpected presence and touched by his thoughtfulness. "Well, there's no sense in standing on the sidewalk freezing, is there?"

"I guess not," Conrad said. He looked deep into Sarah's beautiful eyes. "You're scared."

"I'm scared," she admitted. "Conrad, I know how dangerous British intelligence is. I know how dangerous the CIA is. I know how dangerous every intelligence agency in every country is. I'm not blind. But a man was killed on American soil, and we have a job to do."

"At a very dangerous risk," Conrad pointed out.

"Are you backing down?" she asked, shocked.

"No way." Conrad shook his head. "I know the risks and I accept them," he explained. Casting his eyes around, he studied the sleepy street through the heavily falling snow. The sound of the howling wind sent a strong, melancholy feeling into his heart. "But today I see sadness walking around this town."

Sarah followed his gaze and shivered a little in the gathering cold. "Even on the busy streets of Los Angeles, you can hear the sadness," she told Conrad in a tired voice. "Doesn't matter how crowded the sidewalks are, there is always a pair of sad, desperate eyes somewhere, hungering to be loved...needed..."

Conrad focused his eyes on Sarah's cold face. "Are you okay?" he asked.

"Sure," she said, and forced a weak smile to her shivering lips. "Let me make that pot of coffee I promised you and then let's get to the station, okay? Before we freeze."

"Okay." Conrad made another quick visual check of the street. Somewhere, hidden within the small, snowy town, lurked a darkness that held no conscience—a darkness whose only purpose was to kill and destroy.

CHAPTER FOUR

"I'll be there," Conrad said and ended his call with Mr. Pence. "Well," he said, leaning back in his office chair with a dry grin, "are you up for a road trip?"

"In this weather?" Sarah shook her head no. "I would prefer to stay in town."

Conrad folded his hands behind his head. "Mr. Pence won't talk to me over the phone. He insists that I travel to Yellowstone."

Sarah walked to the office window and took a cautious view of the front street. The snow was falling from the sky in steady, powerful drifts. "Well, we would have to drive. There's no way anyone will fly us down to Anchorage to catch a flight, that's for sure. Not in this weather."

"Hungry?" Conrad asked.

"Not really," Sarah answered absently. Her eyes were focused on the street lamp in front of the police station. It was casting a yellowish light down onto the snow that reminded Sarah of the street lights in her neighborhood back in Los Angeles. Memories of sitting in the kitchen of her old house, sipping coffee and reading a good novel while waiting for her husband to return home, flooded her mind. "Times were good then," she whispered.

"What?"

"Huh?" Sarah turned away from the window.

"What did you say?" Conrad asked.

"Oh, nothing," Sarah said, momentarily flustered. She walked to the chair in front of Conrad's desk and sat down. "I know you haven't been away from New York very long, but do you miss it? The sounds, the lights, the buildings, the people, the restaurants?"

Conrad considered Sarah's question for a moment. "I don't miss the crime, the traffic, the pollution, the dirty streets, the gangs, the violence, the drugs, the high cost of living...those things I don't miss."

"I miss seeing the palm trees swaying in the wind...the smell of the Pacific...the sights of the canyons...a little diner I used to eat at all the time that overlooked a little beach that hardly anyone ever visited. I miss seeing the city lit up at night...a city that—somehow—always captivated me."

Conrad nodded his head. "New York was like that for me. I never tired of walking down Broadway or eating at this little Italian restaurant...a real hole-in-the-wall place that had the best veal parmesan you ever tasted." Conrad smiled. "There was a bookstore called Page After Page that Old Lady Reed used to operate. The bookstore was nothing grand, really, but, I don't know...there was something compelling about the inside of the store that always felt like...home, in a way."

"What happened to the bookstore?" Sarah asked.

"Some loser doped up on drugs held the store up and shot Old Lady Reed in the shoulder. After that, she closed down and moved to Florida with her husband. Now the bookstore is a pawn shop," Conrad said, his voice a mix of anger and sadness. "That's life, I guess."

Sarah grew silent and listened to the winds howl outside. "I admit, I do miss Los Angeles. I guess I would still be living in my old house if my husband and I were still married. After the divorce...well, I felt that it was time for a change in my life. My writing career is stable and my book sales are in the green right now."

Conrad examined Sarah's face. "You're homesick," he said.

Sarah nodded. "I guess I am homesick," she admitted.

"But I could never go back and live in Los Angeles. I know this might sound crazy, but this little town is growing on me. I like my little cabin. I like my coffee shop. I like the snow. I like...being so far away from everything I once knew. I feel that I can...see clearly, somehow. But yes, I am homesick for my old memories."

"I understand." Conrad leaned forward. "Listen, you can back out of this case at any time and take a trip to Los Angeles. Take Amanda with you. I know she would enjoy the trip."

"No," Sarah said firmly. "We're on a case together. Now, what little tidbits did this Mr. Pence give you?"

Conrad shook his head at Sarah. "Stubborn," he said with a laugh and leaned back in his chair. "Mr. Pence didn't say much, but he did manage to convey that Charlie Raymond requested a transfer right after a group of scientists left Yellowstone."

"Scientists? What type of scientists?"

"Pence didn't say," Conrad replied. "The man seemed extremely worried that he had let that bit of information slip. So my guess is that these scientists might be who this Bradley man is searching for."

"Very possible," Sarah said hopefully. "Speaking of Charlie Raymond, how are our three park rangers managing in the holding cell?"

"Last time I checked, they were okay. But we have to remember that any one of those three park rangers could be involved in his murder."

"Not Dave," Sarah protested. "Conrad, Dave—"

Conrad held up his right hand. "I don't think Dave is involved either," he reassured her. "But we have to treat him as a suspect in front of the other two."

Sarah nodded. "Okay," she said, "so what about this trip to Yellowstone? It could be a setup."

"I don't think so. Mr. Pence sounded very nervous, so I did some checking on him." Conrad cleared his throat. "He is married and has three sons and four grandchildren. He and his wife like to take trips to Africa. He's been an employee of the National Park Service at Yellowstone Park for over thirty years. The only legal trouble the man has ever gotten into was when he was nineteen and got arrested for protesting a company that made some toxic house paint. The man is a real 'Keep the Earth Clean' type guy."

Sarah considered this. "So his record seems clean," she said. She pondered for a moment, then switched tracks as something occurred to her. "You know, Yellowstone is home to the largest super volcano in the world," she said worriedly. "What did Charlie Raymond find out that got him killed? Could it have something to do with that?"

"Are you suggesting that the volcano beneath

Yellowstone could erupt?" Conrad asked hesitantly. "Sarah, that's really stretching it."

"I'm not suggesting anything of the sort," Sarah replied. "But I am saying Charlie Raymond was murdered shortly after he transferred to Alaska *and* shortly after a group of scientists left Yellowstone. And the super volcano is the biggest natural threat waiting to happen. Maybe that's the connection."

Conrad rubbed his rough chin. Sarah's theory held merit. It was obvious that Charlie Raymond was murdered for a certain reason—and with MI-6 in town searching for the people who had murdered the man, Conrad saw red flags popping up everywhere. "We have to go down to Yellowstone and talk with Mr. Pence, Sarah. We can't move forward until we do."

"Shouldn't we wait for Raymond's autopsy report?" Sarah suggested. "I'm sure the report will give us a lead or two."

"The coroner can call me with the results. I have to go to Yellowstone. I would like it if you accompanied me."

Sarah leaned forward and picked up a bottle of water from the desk. "If we leave town, Mr. Bradley might suspect something...then again, if we leave town, he might just think we're standing down."

"It's a flip of the coin," Conrad pointed out.

Sarah took a drink of water. It was delicious in her mouth and cold going down her throat. “Okay, Detective Spencer,” she said. “I’ll go to Yellowstone with you. Speaking with Mr. Pence is very important to our case.”

“It’s like my grandmother used to say,” Conrad said. “Whenever I got sick as a kid, she used to insist that I eat matzo ball soup, even though we’re not Jewish. I would always ask her if the soup would make me feel better, and my grandmother would reply ‘It can’t hurt’.”

“That’s true,” Sarah smiled and looked at the phone on Conrad’s desk. “I’d better call Amanda.”

Conrad leaned forward and slid the phone toward Sarah. She set down the water bottle and called Amanda’s home phone. It was picked up on the first ring. “Ms. Garland, how nice of you to call.”

Sarah’s blood froze and her eyes grew wide as panic struck her chest. She recognized the calm British voice. Bradley Preston.

“What...where is Amanda?” she demanded.

“Right here beside me on her cozy brown couch,” Bradley replied easily. “Speak,” he commanded Amanda.

“I’m alive,” Amanda yelled at the phone in a scared voice.

Bradley drew in a breath and slowly exhaled. “Your friend has a lovely home. Reminds me of a flat I had back in London.”

"If you hurt Amanda I will dedicate my life—" Hearing this, Conrad stood up and rushed around his desk. Sarah made room for him to hear Bradley speaking through the receiver.

"Please, Ms. Garland, we are both professionals," Bradley said in a sour voice. "Threats are futile and only serve to create needless enemies."

"What do you want?" Sarah asked.

"Insurance. I want you to leave town now, along with Detective Spencer. You two may return in one week. By then, my job will be accomplished and I will be gone. No one will get hurt and everyone will be none the wiser."

"And Amanda?" Sarah asked.

"If you do as I have requested, no harm will come to her," Bradley assured her. "If you refuse, or decide to play any games, then perhaps a certain man may return back from London only to find himself...wifeless."

"Leave town," Amanda cried out. "Sarah, take Conrad and go on holiday for crying out loud. Do I have to spell it out for you? Bradley is here in my house with a hired killer and a gun and a silencer. Let him have what he wants."

"Do we have an agreement?" Bradley asked.

Conrad nodded at Sarah. "Yes," Sarah said, in a

purposefully defeated tone. "You win, Mr. Bradley. Detective Spencer and I will leave town for one week."

"Beginning tonight," Bradley said forcefully. "I realize the weather is not very favorable, but the sooner the better, I would say."

"Fine, tonight."

"I have a man watching the police station. He will ensure that you keep your word. You have two hours. If you fail to leave town within that time limit, then I will be forced to punish your friend for every minute you delay," Bradley continued.

"Fine, two hours," Sarah agreed quickly. "Please, there is no need to hurt Amanda. She's innocent. Detective Spencer and I will get out of town, okay?"

"Very good, Ms. Garland. You have two hours," Bradley said again and ended the call.

"I'm going to take that man down," Sarah said, slamming the phone down with a furious hand. "This is personal, now. No one messes with my girl and gets away with it."

"Before your head explodes," Conrad said, "we'd better get out of here. We'll take your Subaru. Let's go."

Sarah grabbed Conrad's arm. "Bradley doesn't know you've spoken to Mr. Pence, Conrad. If he finds out, he may hurt Amanda."

"It's a flip of the coin," Conrad reminded Sarah in a steady tone. "We have a hostage being held by a man who will not hesitate to act. Our only chance to save Amanda is to get to Mr. Pence and see what he has to say."

"And then what?" Sarah asked anxiously.

"And then," Conrad said, pulling Sarah up to her feet, "we make an attack plan. Now let's move. We have less than two hours now and the way the snow is falling outside, we're going to need every single second to get out of Snow Falls."

Sarah looked toward the office window. "Hang tight, June Bug...I'm coming back," she promised and then hurried out of the office with Conrad.

CHAPTER FIVE

Conrad and Sarah walked into a warm office that resembled the interior of a log cabin. A wooden desk covered with files and papers stood facing a blazing fire singing in a stone fireplace. The walls of the office were hung with family photos. The floor was decorated with a simple but tasteful green rug. "Please, sit down," Roger Pence said in a welcoming tone.

Sarah walked to a wooden chair with a green cushioned seat, sat down, and smoothed out her dark gray dress. Conrad sat down in the chair next to her. "Thank you for seeing us, Mr. Pence."

Roger looked at Sarah. The woman was beautiful and obviously very brilliant, he observed. With her hair covered by a pink beret and her black leather jacket, she conveyed a certain toughness in her personality. Conrad, on the other hand, looked unkempt in his wrinkled black suit. "I have no more than ten minutes. I'm a very busy man."

Conrad folded his arms. The small, thin man sitting behind the wooden desk reminded him of a boy he had known in grade school. Roger Pence had narrow eyes and a thin, tight face that didn't seem to understand how to smile. He was nearly bald, and currently he bore the expression of someone very constipated. "Sure," Conrad said.

Roger nervously adjusted his gray suit and focused on Sarah and Conrad. "I'm sorry," he said, "I know you two are investigating the murder of a very good man. Charlie Raymond was one of the best. Caring, smart, outgoing...great with the public...always had a joke to tell. Everyone liked him."

"That's not the story his co-workers in Alaska told us," Conrad said. "The report we were given indicated that Mr. Raymond was a cold fish."

Roger's eyes widened and he shook his head. "No, no," he insisted, "Charlie was a delightful man. I admit that I don't smile very often...I blame my mother for that...but Charlie always brought out a smile in me."

"Mr. Pence, you mentioned that Mr. Raymond requested a transfer to Alaska after a group of scientists left Yellowstone?" Sarah asked.

Roger tensed up. "Look," he said worriedly, "that was a

slip of the tongue." He leaned forward and retrieved a piece of peppermint out of a crystal candy dish. "Peppermint?" he offered.

"Speak to us," Conrad told Roger in a tough voice. "We need answers."

Roger popped the peppermint into his mouth and then nervously began to rub his hands together. "Detective Spencer," he said, "I..."

"You're scared," Sarah said.

Surprised, Roger bit down on the peppermint in his mouth so hard it sounded as if he'd cracked a tooth. "I'm leery," he told Sarah.

"Why?" Conrad asked.

Roger continued to rub his hands together. "Detectives," he said, "the scientists who visited Yellowstone were not American. They were British. They visited ostensibly as nothing more than mere tourists. They took a tour of the Old Faithful geyser, visited the hot springs...normal tourist stuff. Charlie, rest his soul, took the group of scientists out each day. They stayed for four days and then left."

"How many scientists?" Conrad asked.

"Three. Two men and one woman."

"Did these scientists mention their field of study?" Sarah inquired.

"They were volcanologists," Roger explained, "on what they called a 'holiday' from their station in Iceland."

"Do you have their names?" Conrad probed.

Roger stopped rubbing his hands, closed his eyes, chewed on his peppermint, and then—painfully, as if he were having his appendix removed at that very moment—nodded his head. "Here," he said and pulled out something from the top left drawer of his desk. "Take this."

Conrad reached forward and accepted the white piece of paper from Roger. The paper held the names of the three scientists. "Gwen...Gregory...Edward."

Sarah studied the names. "This list has their names, the numbers to the cabins they rented, their payment information, their vehicle information...thank you, Mr. Pence, this will be very helpful."

"Mr. Pence," Conrad said, "did Charlie Raymond come to you at any time and express concern over these visitors?"

Roger looked from Conrad to Sarah and hesitated briefly before continuing. "On the fourth day, Charlie did come to me," Roger said and looked down at his hands. "He told me he had seen one of the male scientists taking photos of Old Faithful. Of course, photos are allowed, but Charlie told me this scientist was taking enormous quantities of photos. But that wasn't all...Charlie said that all three scientists had been continuously taking tons of photos of the park, but in continuous shifts. Charlie..."

"Charlie what?" Sarah pressed.

"Charlie told me that he suspected that they were spies for a foreign government. Of course, I laughed him out of my office and told him he had been working too hard," Roger said in an ashamed voice. "And now, he's dead. I should have seen the red flag waving in the air when Charlie put in for an immediate transfer to Alaska. Charlie loved Yellowstone. This park was his home."

"Did you happen to get any photos of these people...maybe on a security camera?" Conrad asked in a steady tone.

Roger shrugged his shoulders. "We have live webcams aimed at Old Faithful and a few other locations, and there are security cameras in the park. But Detective, I don't have the technical staff here to locate that footage in the archives."

"Did you ever meet the scientists?" Sarah asked.

"On the day they left, yes," Roger confessed.

"What did they look like?" Conrad prompted.

"The woman was young, maybe in her mid-twenties...very pretty," Roger explained. "She seemed kinda young to be a scientist, but who was I to question her credentials?"

"And the others?" Conrad urged.

"One of the men was also young, about the same age as the girl. The second man was in his mid to late forties...very stern-looking, never smiled once," Roger continued. "The girl had a reddish color to her hair...the young male had a military type haircut and a face that looked tough as a rock, even though he did smile a little and even shook my hand. The older man, he had on a Minnesota Twins baseball cap when we met, so I couldn't see his hair color. They were all wearing the same type of clothes...kinda like you, Detective Garland. Black and gray."

"Was Charlie Raymond with you when you met them?" Sarah asked.

Roger nodded his head. "He was," he said, "but Charlie wasn't acting like himself. He was nervous and seemed very anxious for the three scientists to leave the park. His face was pale and uneasy. In all my years, I had never seen Charlie so uptight. The scientists obviously noticed this because they all gave Charlie this kind of strange look and then...they left."

"Where did you meet them?" Conrad asked.

"At the Old Faithful geyser. I was there with my

grandson when Charlie came over. He told me the three scientists wanted to take one last look at the geyser before they left."

"Did you see any of them take any photos?"

"The young girl," Roger said, nodding his head. "She was taking photos of the younger guy standing in front of the geyser. I didn't think anything of it. But obviously Charlie did. He frowned at me but didn't say a word."

Conrad looked over at Sarah and then refocused on Roger. "Mr. Pence, you have been a great help to us. Please, if you see these three people, stay away from them and immediately call the police."

"They killed poor Charlie, didn't they?" Roger asked sorrowfully.

"It's possible," Sarah said as she stood up. "Mr. Pence, for now, please do not speak to anyone about our meeting, not even your wife. Detective Spencer and I are going to return to Alaska and continue our investigation."

Roger nervously rose to his feet. "Trust me," he promised, "this meeting never took place. If I ever see those three phonies back here, I'm calling the feds."

"Good idea," Conrad said. He shook Roger's hand. "Thank you for all of your help."

"I'll walk you out," Roger said, sounding relieved. When he reached his office door, he paused. "I was hesitant to speak to you...you have to know what I did today was for the sake of Charlie Raymond, bless his heart. He deserves justice."

"Justice will prevail," Sarah promised as she exited the office.

Conrad shook Roger's hand again and stepped out into the hallway, which smelled of pine and roses. It was immaculately clean and had interesting artwork on the walls that reminded Conrad of spaghetti for some reason. "Let's go get a bite to eat. We have a long drive back to Alaska."

"Sure," Sarah agreed, "I could use something in my stomach. I'm really worried about Amanda, though, Conrad. I want to get back home as soon as possible."

"Let's not be too hasty," Conrad warned her as they began walking down the hallway together. "You and I both know these phony scientists are more likely to be terrorists than spies. Maybe Charlie Raymond realized this, somehow...and managed to extract information about their plans...and he was killed."

Sarah walked into the warm front lobby, made her way to the stone fireplace, and warmed her hands. Conrad grew silent. Sarah smiled at the older lady sitting behind the wooden front desk. "Very cold outside," she said. The woman smiled back but didn't reply. Instead, she went back to reading the old Western novel in front of her.

Conrad nodded his head toward the set of double glass doors. "Ready?"

Sarah kept her eye on the older lady. "It sure seems strange without Charlie around, doesn't it?"

The mention of Charlie's name made the woman lower her book. "You know Charlie?" she asked Sarah.

"Sure, Charlie is a fine man," Sarah smiled. "I was sad to hear that he transferred out of the park."

She put down her book and clasped her hands together. Her graceful features took on a very sour expression. "Charlie was run off," she said, looking toward the hallway. "I don't care who hears me say that either. Charlie was run off from here. Shameful it was."

"Why would someone as nice as Charlie be run off?" Sarah asked with concern.

The older lady kept her eyes on the hallway. "Mr. Pence ran Charlie off. Why? Because Charlie called the FBI, that's why. Charlie was afraid that our park was under surveillance. The FBI came and left, and when they left, Charlie left. Whoever they were, they covered up their tracks too well. But I know the truth...Mr. Pence ran Charlie off."

"How awful," Sarah said.

The older woman nodded her head in agreement. "Mr. Pence said he forced Charlie to transfer for the good of the park...maybe that was so, but that still doesn't excuse how poor Charlie was treated."

"Oh, I'm so sorry," Sarah said.

"Me, too," the receptionist said and picked up her book again. "I just work here part-time to supplement my Social Security income. But you'd better bet your butter beans I'm applying elsewhere, since that happened."

Sarah looked at Conrad to see if he had heard this. He raised his eyebrows and then nodded his head toward the front doors again. "Ready?"

"Take care," Sarah said to the older woman and followed Conrad out into the parking lot. It was surrounded with breathtakingly tall trees covered with winter snow. "So Charlie called the FBI, and that might have alerted Bradley Preston. And his transfer to Alaska might not have been so selfless after all."

"Seems that way, doesn't it?" Conrad said, taking in the sight of the soaring trees. Beyond the trees lay a rough and rugged landscape of geysers, hot springs, rock formations, and other natural wonders that attracted millions of tourists each year. But what Conrad thought about the most was the volcano under their feet. Even though it wasn't visible, he knew it was below them, growling, hissing, bubbling, anxious to explode at any moment. "Let's get out of here, okay?"

"Sure," Sarah agreed. She pointed at the red BMW

parked next to her Subaru. "I guess Mr. Pence does okay for himself."

Conrad walked toward the car and examined the flashy red car, which was in a reserved parking spot with Roger Pence's name stenciled in neat letters on the curb. "This car is brand-new," he told Sarah. Stooping over, he looked in the driver's side window to examine the interior. "Clean as a whistle, too."

"I would bet my last book advance Mr. Pence was paid a pretty penny to push Charlie Raymond out of Yellowstone," Sarah said. Looking around, she spotted a young woman wearing a park ranger uniform watching them. "Let's go."

Conrad lifted his head and, following Sarah's gaze, spotted the park ranger standing next to a tall, snow-covered tree at the south end of the parking lot. He offered her a quick, friendly wave and walked over to Sarah's Subaru. "Ten bucks Mr. Pence is being eaten up with guilt. With some people it's like that," he said, climbing into the passenger seat and buckling up.

Sarah walked around to the driver's side, glanced over her shoulder, and saw the park ranger pulling a cell phone out of the pocket of her brown coat. "Hurry up and tell Mr. Pence we're leaving, young lady," she whispered as she pulled open the car door. "Our friend over there is calling Mr. Pence," she informed Conrad.

"I expected him to have a set of eyes on us," Conrad replied as Sarah situated herself behind the steering wheel and buckled her seat belt.

"Years back," Sarah said, bringing her Subaru to life, "my ex-husband and I visited this park. We had a wonderful time. We watched Old Faithful erupt, slept in a rented RV, roasted marshmallows over an open fire. Our time here was very nice."

Conrad waited until Sarah had pulled away from the main administration building before he spoke. "Memories hurt," he said, watching the tall trees roll past the Subaru, slowly at first, and then faster and faster as the vehicle gained speed and headed up the Mammoth Hot Springs road toward the north entrance.

"Yes, they do," Sarah agreed. "Conrad?"

"Yeah?"

"Why Alaska? Mr. Pence said Charlie Raymond applied for a transfer, but his gossipy receptionist insists Mr. Pence ran him off."

"It's possible Charlie was given a choice...transfer to a new post or get canned," Conrad pointed out. "Realizing that he was in danger, maybe he chose a remote post hoping that he could escape and stay hidden."

"Which means someone here at Yellowstone told those three phony scientists where Charlie Raymond transferred to, right? How else could they have located the man? And because he called the FBI, which most likely alerted British intelligence, Mr. Bradley jumped into the game, tracked down Charlie Raymond's new location, and knew the killers would make a beeline for Alaska."

"So Mr. Bradley did the same, hoping to catch the killers before they killed Charlie," Conrad added. "Which means Mr. Bradley must have known Charlie's location was somehow leaked by someone right here at Yellowstone."

"By Mr. Pence?"

Conrad rubbed his chin and surveyed the beautiful, dangerous landscape whizzing past the Subaru's windows. "Most likely," he said. "It's possible the killers left the park after their little tourist charade, then doubled back and had a little one-on-one talk with Mr. Pence. It's possible they're the ones who paid for his new BMW, too."

"Our three fake scientists could have threatened Mr. Pence, pushing him into a corner, forcing him to make Charlie agree to a transfer. Now, because Charlie is dead, Pence is being eaten alive by guilt."

"And it just so happens that Charlie was transferred to a very remote park that doesn't get much foot traffic, especially in the winter season," Conrad added. Before he could continue, his cell phone rang. "Turn down the heat," he told Sarah as he checked the incoming caller. "It's the coroner...about time."

Sarah reached forward and adjusted a black knob on the dashboard. The heat blowing noisily from the vents slowed and hushed. "Let's see what information we get this morning," she said.

Conrad placed the call on speakerphone. "Detective Spencer."

"Detective Spencer, this is Dr. Ford Jenkins," an old man's voice came from the speakers. "You don't know me."

"I can't say that I do."

"My office is located in Anchorage," Dr. Jenkins continued. "The body of Charlie Raymond was sent to me for further examination by your local coroner, and—"

"What was the man's cause of death, Dr. Jenkins?" Conrad asked, getting straight to the point. Sarah bit down on her lower lip and waited.

"Charlie Raymond was shot with a dart containing a highly lethal poison," Dr. Jenkins said, sounding annoyed by the interruption.

"Yes, but what was the poison that killed him?"

"The poison is not yet identified," he said. "Further lab

tests and mass spectrometry may reveal the precise chemical formulation, but that takes time," he said with not a small amount of condescension.

"I see," Conrad said.

"The poison," Dr. Jenkins said, with a pause for the click of what sounded like a very expensive lighter and the unmistakable sound of a puff from a no doubt very expensive cigar, "is extremely lethal."

"I kinda figured that out for myself, doc," Conrad replied in exasperation, realizing that the man he was speaking to was nothing more than a conceited snob.

"The poison," Dr. Jenkins continued his patronizingly slow explanation, "attacks the victim's heart. Once the poison reaches the heart, the heart muscle immediately ceases to function and the subject suffers instant cardiac arrest. Very merciful, actually."

"A man is dead," Conrad said impatiently. "I don't think having his life snatched away was very merciful."

"Detective Spencer," Dr. Jenkins began to reply and then stopped abruptly. The unmistakable sounds of a scuffle crackled over the speaker phone. "Who are you...what are you...hey! Who do you think..." and then the call went dead.

"Dr. Jenkins?" Conrad yelled into his cell phone. "Dr. Jenkins, are you there?"

"They got to him," Sarah said in shock. "It had to be MI-6."

Conrad tossed his cell phone into his lap. "By the end of the day, if not already, Charlie Raymond's identity will be completely erased from every database known to man. The man's life will be wiped off the face of the earth, leaving you and me trying to solve the murder of a ghost."

Sarah slowed the Subaru down, taking this in. "So what's our next step, Conrad?" she asked in a desperate voice. "If what you're saying is true, and I think it is, then pursuing this case is futile."

Conrad sat quietly for a few minutes as Sarah drove. Then he turned his head and looked at her with worried eyes. "Maybe we can't pursue a murder case anymore...at this juncture, anyway...but we can still protect the innocent. We'd better make tracks back to Snow Falls."

Sarah turned her head and read Conrad's eyes. "Oh no," she said as alarm gripped her heart. "Mr. Bradley...he'll kill everyone who was aware of Charlie Raymond."

"Including Mr. Pence," Conrad said as he grabbed his cell phone. He dialed Roger Pence's office. "Pick up, man, pick up."

"Detective Spencer?" Mr. Pence answered his phone.

"Listen to me," Conrad said hurriedly, "get out of your office and hide. Your life is in danger. Detective Garland

and I know you pushed Charlie Raymond into that transfer and—"

"I..." Roger started to object but caved in to his fear. "Yes, okay...it's true. But I didn't have a choice. I was threatened and so was my family. But...Charlie...poor Charlie...I swear, Detective Spencer, I didn't want any harm to come to him. I haven't had a wink of sleep since I heard that he was killed."

"We'll talk about that some other time," Conrad told him. "Right now, get to your family and get them into hiding."

"I have a girl outside watching my office," Roger said. "I've informed all the park rangers to alert me if they spot anyone matching the description of the three people responsible for Charlie's death. I'm safe in my office."

"No, you're not," Conrad snapped. "Get out of your office, get to your family, and go into hiding. I'll call you when it's safe to come out. Now go!"

"I...yes, okay," Roger said and hung up.

"Think he listened?" Sarah asked Conrad.

"For his sake, he'd better have," Conrad said. "Hey, my stomach is really grumbling. I'm not going to be any good unless we stop and eat somewhere."

"Let me at least get us farther west into Montana," Sarah countered.

"Good idea," Conrad reluctantly agreed. "We'll have time to see if anyone is following us."

"Could you call Amanda for me? You know the number," Sarah said, focusing on the road. The sides of the road were covered in heavy snow, but the road itself was well salted and cleared of snow. Even with the roads clear, Sarah didn't want to turn the road trip into a desperate race. Instead, she drove with caution.

"Bradley could still be there. I don't think that's a good idea."

"Please," Sarah begged. "Conrad, it's been days. I...have to know if my friend is still...alive."

Conrad understood. Against his better judgment, he dialed Amanda's home phone. To his shock, she picked up. "Are you okay?" he asked her, placing the call on speakerphone.

"I'm fine, for now," Amanda said in a scared voice. Sarah and Conrad heard her take a shaky sigh and exchanged a glance. "Bradley and another bloke with him left my house as soon as you and Sarah left town," Amanda continued. "I was ordered to remain in my home."

Sarah felt tears begin to flow as soon as she heard Amanda's voice. "I'm so sorry I had to leave you."

"Don't be sorry," Amanda began to cry. "I was the one

who left you, remember? If only we had stayed together...as partners."

"We're on our way back right now," said Sarah, trying to keep her eyes from blurring with tears. "Right now we're in southern Montana. We went and talked with Charlie Raymond's supervisor at Yellowstone."

"Bradley hasn't been back to your home since Sarah and I drove out of town?" Conrad asked.

"Not a peep," Amanda replied with a quiet sniffle. "I thought of making a run for it, but then I have to think about my Jack. I've got my boots on, I even put on my warmest sweater and wool dress, and I'm ready to dash out the back door at any second. But...I can't."

"Stay put, June Bug," Sarah pleaded.

"Do I really have a choice? I'm trapped," Amanda said pointedly. "Before Bradley left he also...mentioned my son. I'm not stepping foot out of my home."

Conrad knew it was not humanly possible to understand the fear and anger and desperation Amanda was feeling. "I promise to get this guy," he told her.

Amanda laughed humorlessly. "You promise to take down a powerful British agent? That's a laugh, Conrad. No offense, I know you're a decent bloke and all, but you're in way over your head."

"Maybe not," Conrad said. "Listen to me. I'm going to

give you three names. Wrap your memory around these names and use them as a weapon if you can."

"What names?"

"The names of the three people who killed Charlie Raymond," Conrad explained. He motioned to Sarah to turn off the noisy heating completely. "The people Bradley Preston is pursuing. My hunch is that they are still in Snow Falls because they plan to eliminate anyone Charlie Raymond might have confided in. And trust me when I say this: Bradley Preston is going to do that exact thing. Preston is going to kill anyone who even remotely knew Charlie Raymond, and he especially isn't going to let anyone live who saw the man's dead body."

"Oh dear," Amanda said. "Sarah? Is this true?"

"Conrad is right," Sarah said miserably. "It seems that Bradley Preston is after a group of terrorists who might have been planning an attack on Yellowstone National Park. Charlie Raymond uncovered their plot and was killed. At least, this is the conclusion Conrad and I have reached."

"Not only that, but Charlie Raymond was pushed out of his job at Yellowstone by his supervisor," Conrad jumped in. "He was sent to Alaska to die. I guess he knew his time was short and that's why he went out to the lake to meet Dave. I think he was going to confide in Dave, and would have if Dave had arrived on time."

"I think Charlie knew he was going to die and wore his uniform to the lake because he wanted to die the way a soldier does in combat, proud and brave," Sarah added.

"Well, I'm glad he went with honor, but that doesn't make his death any less awful," Amanda replied sadly. "And I still don't know what to think or what to do. There's a powerful snowstorm raging out there, my snowmobile needs a new spark plug. My truck will never make it through this snow and you know I'm simply lousy on skis. And even if I had to make a run for it, where would I go?" Amanda's voice tugged at Sarah's heart. But suddenly, her friend exclaimed, "Oh, hang on, yes!"

"What?" Sarah asked, alarmed.

"If I'm going to die, I'm not going to make it easy for them to find me. Jack wouldn't allow me to just sit idly by and wait to have a bullet with my afternoon tea. I know where I can run and hide."

Sarah struggled to catch up to Amanda's train of thought. When she did, a quick smile touched her lips. "Don't forget the kitten, and leave when it gets dark."

"There's a blasted snowstorm outside," Amanda said, exasperated. "If I wait until night, I'm likely to get myself lost. So here's what I'm going to do. I'm going to call Jack and then I'm going to call my son and tell them what's happening. My son is smart. He'll go into hiding. Jack, he'll do what needs to be done to stay alive...I hope. I just can't sit around in my kitchen any longer and wait for the inevitable to happen. If Bradley Preston intends on killing me, he might very well go after my son and my husband, too. I have to fight."

"Don't call your son or your husband," Conrad blurted out in warning.

"Why not, for crying out loud?" Amanda demanded.

"If you get caught, Bradley may check your cell phone. Even if you erase your calls, he may still be able to track them," Conrad explained. "Right now, it's better to stay silent."

"I have to warn my family," Amanda argued.

"If you do, you might get them killed," Conrad said patiently. "Leave your cell phone on your kitchen table, leave your back door wide open, and make it appear that you were abducted."

Amanda didn't speak for a long moment. Sarah could hardly bear the silence as she drove on, waiting for her friend's reply. There was no forcing a difficult decision in a crisis. Sarah willed her dear friend to grasp the hope offered by Conrad's solid, trustworthy presence. It was the one thing Sarah knew to be true and real.

Just when Sarah was beginning to despair, Amanda spoke again. "Okay, Conrad, I'll make it seem like someone grabbed me. I...trust you."

Conrad smiled with relief. "Sarah and I are on our way."

Sarah decided to throw caution to the wind and pressed down harder on the gas pedal. "If Bradley hasn't returned for you, that must mean he hasn't found the three people who killed Charlie Raymond," she told Amanda. "So listen to Conrad and remember the names he's about to give you. If you're caught, use the names as a weapon...tell Bradley you sent the names to the press along with information about Charlie Raymond."

Conrad drew in a deep breath and spoke the names of the three people Charlie Raymond had escorted around Yellowstone National Park. "Remember them."

"I already have them memorized," Amanda promised. "Okay, guys, I'm...going to make my move on the chessboard...I love you both."

"We love you too," Sarah said, feeling tears burst from her eyes. "Amanda...June Bug...run as fast as you can and don't stop."

"I will," Amanda assured her. "Conrad, when you get back in town, remember that I owe you a cup of coffee," she said and ended the call.

Sarah pressed down even harder on the gas pedal. "We've got to get back to Snow Falls," she said in an urgent voice.

"Alive, not dead," Conrad reminded her. "Slow down, okay?"

Reluctantly, Sarah eased up on the gas. "Bradley gave us a week...it's been three days. I told Amanda that he hasn't found his targets yet. The truth is, Bradley could have already found his targets and now he's preparing to strike at anyone who remains a threat to him."

"Why did he give us a week?" Conrad wondered aloud as he looked out of the passenger side window. "How could he be certain he would be able to track down Charlie Raymond's killers in only a week? And why was he at the lake? I'm sure that gray thread Andrew found belongs to Bradley." Conrad grew silent for a minute as his mind struggled through a messy room of questions. "Maybe..."

"Maybe what?"

"Step on it!" Conrad exclaimed. "We've got no time to lose."

Sarah didn't argue. She stepped on the gas pedal and sent her Subaru racing down the highway. As she sped through Montana, she listened to Conrad's careful explanation of what he thought was happening in Snow Falls. Every single word Conrad spoke struck tremendous fear into her heart.

CHAPTER SIX

Amanda unlocked the back door to Sarah's coffee shop and eased quietly into the kitchen. Leaving the lights off, she crouched down and duck-walked to the office with the little kitten cradled in her arms. "We're going to be okay," she promised the kitten in a whisper. But when she entered the dark office, her heart nearly stopped. Someone was sitting in the corner, breathing hard.

"Help...me," a desperate voice pleaded. The voice was that of a young woman.

"Who are you?" Amanda demanded. "What are you doing here?"

"My name is...Gwen Palmer. Please help me...I've been shot..."

"Oh dear," Amanda said. Feeling fear claw at her chest,

she set the kitten down on Sarah's desk and squatted next to Gwen. She couldn't see much in the dark, but she could smell blood. "Where are you hurt?"

"My...shoulder," Gwen moaned in pain.

Amanda agonized, torn by compassion but also something darker and more threatening that she couldn't ignore. "Why should I help you? You killed Charlie Raymond."

"No," Gwen pleaded, breathless with pain, "we came here to try and save him, but Bradley got to him first. Your accent...you're British?"

"Yes," Amanda confirmed.

"What's your name?"

"Amanda."

"Amanda, my name is Agent Gwen Palmer. I'm with MI-6. My partners and I have been tracking Bradley Preston."

Amanda pressed a hand against her forehead in shock and confusion. "That awful man threatened my family. He threatened my son and my husband."

Gwen pushed her sweaty black hair away from her eyes. She looked overheated in her thick blue ski suit which had an ominous dark stain at the shoulder. "Bradley will kill anyone who gets in his way. Just like Charlie Raymond got in his way."

"I don't understand."

"I can't explain...not now. Please, I need help," Gwen begged. "The bullet...went straight through my shoulder, but it hurts..."

Amanda balled her hands into tight fists, closed her eyes, let out a silent scream, and then took a very deep breath. She kicked the office door shut with one foot, stood up, and hit the light switch. The bright overhead lights revealed a very beautiful young woman struggling to hold her left shoulder. "I will help you, but if you try anything funny I swear I'll stuff your face into a snowbank."

Gwen tried to nod her head but fainted before she could. Amanda dropped her head to her chest in exasperation. "Well," she said, looking back up at the kitten who was sitting on its haunches wondering what in the world was going on, "this is just the cherry on the cake, now isn't it, little guy?" The kitten let out a quiet meow. "I'd better save this girl's life. Even without that ski suit I think she may be running a high fever."

Two hours later, Gwen regained consciousness. She came to on the office floor with her ski suit removed, and immediately reached down with her right hand and felt that her gun, which had been concealed in a shoulder holster, was gone. "Amanda?" Gwen called out cautiously.

"I'm right here," Amanda said. Standing with her back to the office door, she watched Gwen struggle to lift her head. "You were right; the bullet went straight through. I found the entry and exit wounds. I washed the wounds with peroxide, covered them with some bandages, and put your arm in a homemade sling I made out of dish towels. I also managed to get some aspirin into you while you were asleep."

"Thank you," Gwen said gratefully. Even though her head felt fuzzy and her shoulder was crying out in pain, she felt much better than she had before Amanda discovered her.

"Why are you in Sarah Garland's office?" Amanda asked. "How did you get in here?"

"I had to hide," Gwen explained. "I figured this coffee shop would be the last place Bradley would search for me. I was assigned to watch you and Detective Garland."

"By Bradley?"

"Yes," Gwen explained in a pained voice. "After we saw you at the lake."

Amanda shook her head. "I'm not a cop, sister. My brain doesn't wrap around all of this cops and robbers stuff. My friend Sarah can pick a clue out of a haystack with her eyes closed, but I'm not that gifted, so help me out, okay?"

"Biological warfare," Gwen said. Her voice sounded weak. "Bradley Preston is planning to drop a very deadly canister, filled with a lethal virus, into the Old Faithful geyser. A small explosive charge will be attached to the canister, just powerful enough to blow it open. It will be set to detonate when the geyser is predicted to erupt." Gwen closed her eyes. "My partners and I have been working undercover...getting close to Bradley. When we were at Yellowstone...Bradley was with us. He stayed in the shadows. But...Charlie Raymond managed to snap a photo of us talking with Bradley one night..." Gwen struggled to sit upright but clutched at her shoulder and laid back down again, breathing hard.

"Take it easy, girl," Amanda said. "We've got all night."

"We've got very little time left," Gwen warned.

"What do you mean?"

"Bradley is a rogue agent. He's a very deadly man and he wants to attract the attention of some very deadly and powerful organizations abroad...well, somehow he found out that my partners and I were undercover. He's already killed Gregory and Edward...I'm the only one remaining." Gwen winced in pain. "He was supposed to purchase the virus from a seller on March 20th...months away. Somehow Bradley found out we were planning to catch him in the act of purchasing the virus. But somehow...we don't know how...he arranged for the virus to be delivered to Yellowstone earlier than expected. So then he came here to kill Charlie Raymond...knowing I and my partners would follow."

"You said we have very little time. What did you mean by that?" Amanda pressed.

Gwen laid her head back down on the floor. "I overheard Bradley Preston talking on the phone the day he sent Detective Garland and Detective Spencer out of town." She paused, breathing unevenly.

"Don't stop talking now," Amanda said. "My girl, you'd better get your mind up and working."

Gwen closed her eyes. "The virus Bradley Preston is going to release is extremely contagious and deadly. Symptoms of the virus will not begin to appear for at least two weeks and Yellowstone is a major tourist attraction. How many people will become infected at the park...and then spread the virus? How many people will fly on planes, drive hundreds of miles home, or travel out of the country entirely?"

"I get it, I get it," Amanda said, horror dawning on her.

"Bradley sent Detectives Garland and Spencer away because he knew they would pay Mr. Pence a visit at Yellowstone Park...and he planted the virus...the seller would hide it in their car..."

"Oh dear," Amanda said, "the virus...Sarah is carrying it right back to Alaska."

Gwen nodded her head. "When she returns...Bradley is going to kill her and Detective Spencer, along with anyone who knew Charlie Raymond, including you."

"But I didn't know the man," Amanda protested.

"You saw his body," Gwen said. She opened her eyes. "The virus...it dies in the cold. It has to be kept in a special canister. Bradley is going to release it when Yellowstone reaches a suitable temperature for the virus to survive. If he gets the virus and escapes from this town...we'll never see him again."

"But...we can call the FBI...the CIA...Interpol!" Amanda declared.

"Bradley will simply release the virus elsewhere," Gwen said in a defeated voice. "A cruise ship, perhaps?"

"So this sour rat is just waiting for Sarah to return with the canister?"

"Yes."

"Where is he now, Gwen? Can you tell me that?"

"Because I managed to escape...there's no telling where he is hiding now. But...he won't attack until he has the canister in his hands. He won't risk anything until Detective Garland's return."

Amanda moaned miserably. "He never intended to harm my son or husband, did he? Only me."

Gwen closed her eyes and nodded her head. "When you have no emotions, then you can't be threatened. You...love your family and Bradley used your love to weaken you. He also used you to force Detectives Garland and Spencer to leave town."

"Because they love me," Amanda said.

"Yes," Gwen explained. "You are the least of Bradley Preston's worries...but make no mistake...he intends to kill you."

Amanda looked down at the little kitten on Sarah's desk, where it was happily batting around a crumpled receipt. "I have to call Sarah to warn her," she finally spoke. "She and Conrad are driving back as we speak."

"No," Gwen said in an alarmed voice. "The canister has a bomb attached to it. If Bradley suspects that Detective Garland will not return, he'll trigger the bomb remotely. Your friend is driving a great distance. They'll become infected and...unknowingly infect hundreds, if not more."

"Dandy, just dandy," Amanda fretted. "You know, is it so much to ask for a nice hot cup of tea while watching a silly romantic comedy? Huh? Is it? I mean, what is this world coming to? This is Snow Falls, Alaska, for crying out loud.

This is where the polar bears play and the Eskimos live...this isn't supposed to be a place for wacky models who like to build creepy snowmen...or Mr. 'Forget About It' himself along with all his silly sidekicks. My little town is supposed to be a place where a person can eat a custard tart in peace!"

"Wacky models...creepy snowmen...what in the world are you talking about?" Gwen asked.

"Forget it, you wouldn't understand," Amanda sighed. "So I guess all we can do is wait until my friends return and then watch them get filled with bullet holes, is that it?"

"Bradley has a listening device in Detective Garland's Subaru. If you call them, he'll set off the bomb," Gwen explained. "The virus...it won't just infect your friends, it'll spread into the air...there won't be any way of stopping it."

"Well, I'm not going to just sit around and wait for Bradley Preston to kill my friends, me, and other innocent people and then go skipping through the land watching millions of people die. I have to do something." Amanda pressed her hands up against the office door. "Think," she told herself, "think...think..." And then she looked at the little kitten again and smiled. "I think I have a plan," she told Gwen.

Gwen struggled to keep her eyes open. "Please, don't do

anything drastic. I just need a little time to gain my energy back..."

"And do nothing," Amanda pointed out. "Listen, girly, I'm not daft." She pointed at the telephone sitting on Sarah's desk. "If you were an honest little bumblebee, you would have called your people across the pond and they would be swarming all over Alaska and my friends right now. But instead, you have your own agenda. That's why I took your gun and hid it."

Gwen opened her eyes and stared up at Amanda in realization that the woman leaning against the office door wasn't as dim as she first appeared to be.

CHAPTER SEVEN

Sarah didn't like stopping. She was anxious to get back to Snow Falls and find Amanda. But her stomach was crying with hunger and she knew that if she and Conrad didn't eat something substantial they wouldn't be able to make the drive back to Alaska. "It's not likely that Bradley is going to let us just drive down Main Street and unpack our bags in peace," she told Conrad.

"Nope," Conrad agreed as he took a bite of a turkey sandwich. The small roadside diner he and Sarah had stopped at was empty of patrons. A few lone vehicles rushed by on the main road out front, but not one of them stopped. "Snow is picking up," he noted in a worried voice.

Sarah looked out of the window next to their table and studied the falling snow. The outside world appeared so cold and unfriendly, while the inside of the diner felt warm and inviting. The smell of fresh coffee and apple pie filled the air. Even though the diner was small, it was obvious the owner took great pride in his establishment. Cozy as the diner was, though, Sarah felt a prickle of anxiety in her stomach as she looked at the gathering snow outside. "We'd better hit the road."

Conrad pointed at Sarah's half-eaten plate of meatloaf. "Eat," he told her.

Sarah sighed and focused on her food. "Any idea how we're going to get into town without being seen?"

"Yes," said Conrad, finishing his turkey sandwich.

"Well?"

Conrad picked up his glass of water and took a sip. "Our goal now is to save innocent lives. I doubt that pinning the murder of Charlie Raymond on anyone is even possible now. What we need to do is get into attack mode and hit Bradley when he least expects it."

"We're running out of time."

"We have plenty of time," Conrad assured her. "We'll drive in shifts and reach Snow Falls with a full day to spare."

"And what will we do when we get there?" Sarah asked. "Bradley will be waiting for us."

“I know.” Conrad gestured for Sarah to eat while he talked. “We’re going to slip in under the cover of night. I would call Andrew, but the last thing I need is for him to go into panic mode. Andrew is a good man, but he doesn’t have the training to deal with MI-6.”

Sarah took a quick bite of meatloaf and looked back out at the snowy road. “Okay, so we go in under the cover of night. Then what? Bradley isn’t going to make his position known to us. The man will know we’re not coming back to Snow Falls to shake hands with him, Conrad.”

“When we get back into town, we split up. You find Amanda and I’ll go straight to the police station. Bradley can’t hit two locations at once. Once you find Amanda, I want you two to stay in your coffee shop, assuming that’s where she is.”

“She’ll be there,” Sarah assured him.

Conrad nodded. “Bradley went after Charlie Raymond because he came across some very damaging information. We agree on that, right?”

Sarah put down her fork. “Yes,” she agreed.

“And a drive from Snow Falls to Yellowstone and back would take about a week, right?”

“If you’re driving in shifts and make very few stops, maybe even less,” Sarah pointed out.

"And," Conrad continued, "Bradley didn't send us out of town expecting us to go sightseeing at the Grand Canyon. He must have known Yellowstone was our target."

"So he wanted us to go to Yellowstone," Sarah concluded.

Conrad nodded. "But why? That question made me think about what Pence said, about Bradley's people taking all of those photos."

"To plan their terrorist attack," Sarah said. "It has to be."

"I agree...but then why did Bradley let us go to Yellowstone? He wanted us—needed us—to go to Yellowstone, and he used threats to force us out of town."

Sarah dropped her eyes down to her lap and tried to think. "Maybe he wanted us to talk to Mr. Pence. But that doesn't make any sense, does it?"

"No," Conrad said. "Here's what we do know: Bradley sent us away for a reason. When we return, I think it's safe to say he's going to attack."

Sarah shook her head, feeling frustration settle into her mind. "This is bad, Conrad," she said, standing up. "Bradley has the high ground on us."

Conrad rubbed the back of his neck and slowly rose to his feet. "I know," he said, sounding tired. "If we can just figure out why he wanted us to go to Yellowstone..."

Sarah closed her eyes. "He wanted us to believe that the three people Charlie Raymond showed around the park were his enemies...and he asked me to stand down."

"Because Bradley knew he was eventually going to send us to Yellowstone and didn't want us connecting the dots," Conrad pointed out. "He had us looking to the right when we needed to be looking left."

"Okay, so he played a little mind game and led us down the wrong path," Sarah admitted. "But he gave away his position when he ordered us out of town for a week."

Conrad tipped his head to one side as he thought about this. "We're making assumptions here, but yeah, that's the way it seems."

"Okay, so assume Gwen, Gregory, and Edward are a part of Bradley's team and that they're planning a terrorist attack. This means that they aren't really part of MI-6."

Conrad pointed at her brown paper cup of coffee still sitting on the table. "Maybe yes...maybe no," he said, moving toward the front door of the diner. "Remember, Charlie Raymond did call the FBI."

Sarah grabbed her cup of coffee and followed Conrad outside. A gorgeous snow-covered landscape of rocky hills and soaring trees stood before her. For a second, Sarah stood very quietly and absorbed the beauty into her heart. She was struck by the contrast between the stark beauty before her and the complexity of the case in which she found herself and her loved ones tangled so deeply.

She shook her head once to clear her thoughts. "Conrad, are you implying Bradley and his team might be rogue agents?" she said after a moment.

"I'm implying that Bradley could still have the ability to access inside information somehow," Conrad said, walking over to Sarah's Subaru. "I'm—" Conrad suddenly stopped.

"What?" Sarah asked.

"I'm not sure." Conrad stared at the back of the vehicle. "The spare tire attached to the back of your Subaru..."

Conrad reached out to the spare tire and gripped it, pressing in deeply with his fingers. Sarah watched him, curious. Conrad examined the rim of the tire. It was gray with dirt, snow, and salt. "What is it?" she asked.

Conrad turned his attention away from the rim and examined the tire valve stem. With cautious hands, he felt the black cap screwed onto the stem. It appeared to be just an average valve stem cap, but the more Sarah looked at it, the more she saw there was something odd about its shape.

"Tracking device," Conrad said, carefully removing the cap from the tire stem. "I almost didn't see it. I just noticed that the spare tire appeared less full."

Sarah watched Conrad examine the cap. "If there is a tracking device—"

"Then there might be a listening device," Conrad finished with a worried look in his eyes. "Sarah, check the inside of your car."

"You're the one with the eyes of a hawk."

"You'll be fine," Conrad explained, "just be quiet about it."

Sarah nodded, jogged to the driver's side door and pulled it open. With methodical eyes, she began examining the interior of the Subaru as Conrad dropped to his knees to search the underside. The Subaru only allowed room for two seats and a small storage area behind the seats. The storage area held two bags of clothes she and Conrad had purchased on their way to Yellowstone, a case of water, and two pairs of boots. Sarah didn't see anything out of the ordinary.

She reached her hand behind the driver's seat and began feeling the back side of the seat. With a sinking feeling, her fingers found a small bump on the lower part of the seat. Sticking her head farther in, she looked down and saw a small black circle, no bigger than a button, at the very bottom; it was nearly invisible against the black upholstery. Slowly, as if the device were a bomb, she eased out of the Subaru and walked around to the back of the car. "Conrad—"

"Wait a minute," Conrad called out urgently from under the Subaru.

Sarah could only see Conrad's feet sticking out from beneath the car. Seconds later she saw his legs appear, then his stomach, and finally his chest as he inched out from under the vehicle. He held a silver canister in his hand. "Take this," he said.

Sarah reached out and took the canister uneasily. A symbol was stenciled on it in a sickening shade of neon green. She recognized it as the same symbol used for medical waste disposal. "I found the listening device," Sarah said in a hushed voice. "It's behind my seat, near the floor. It wasn't hard to spot."

Conrad scrambled to his feet, brushed snow off his pants, and took the silver canister back from Sarah. "This is why Bradley sent us to Yellowstone...to be his errand boy. Pence...that rat," Conrad cursed.

"Just be grateful," Sarah said. "All this because you thought to check the spare tire."

Conrad stared at the canister in his hand. "This symbol means it contains some type of a biological weapon...a virus, most likely. We have Bradley in the palm of our hands. Now the question is, how do we save our friends?"

Sarah shoved her hands into the pockets of her coat. "We need a plan and I think I have one," she said, feeling her mind go to work. She looked back at the small diner.

"This canister looks just like an old coffee thermos, doesn't it?"

"It sure does," Conrad agreed. He saw the gleam of hope in Sarah's eyes. "All right, Detective Garland, tell me what you're thinking."

Sarah looked away from the diner and glanced up into the heavily falling snow. The snow in Montana felt somehow different than the snow in Alaska, yet it still felt clean and pure. "Bradley is trained in the game of manipulation," she said in a calm tone. "Conrad, you and I understand his game all too well. And now it's time to chase the Queen and get our King out of check." Without saying another word, Sarah lowered her head and headed back to the diner.

Conrad remained at the Subaru, gazing at the canister. He was holding death and misery in his hands—death and misery that a very deadly man wanted to expose to the world. But Conrad felt hope ignite in his chest. He felt that even though he and Sarah had lost a few battles, they were going to win the war.

Ten minutes later, Sarah reappeared carrying an old metal coffee thermos. She waved at Conrad, smiled, and then pointed to an old payphone standing off to the side of the diner. "I need to make a call."

CHAPTER EIGHT

Amanda carefully opened the office door. Leaving Gwen behind, she slipped into the kitchen, hurriedly filled a coffee mug with water, and made her way back to the office. Even though she strongly doubted Gwen's story, she knew letting the woman suffer thirst was cruel. "Here," she said, squatting down, "take a drink."

Gwen leaned up on her good elbow and, with Amanda's help, managed to take a few sips of water. "Thank you."

"Don't thank me for anything," Amanda said sourly. "You were going to partake in the killing of millions of people."

"No, you don't understand," Gwen desperately tried to explain. "I really do work for MI-6. I haven't contacted my superior because...if my superior finds out that I failed, I might as well be dead."

"Why?"

Gwen closed her eyes. "It's complicated."

"Life is complicated, my girl. Try me."

"Bradley Preston is not just a rogue agent, he's also the brother of a very powerful operative within British intelligence. My partners and I were assigned to Bradley under strict secrecy. No one is supposed to even know he's alive. But my superior...don't ask for his name...he couldn't stand by and let Bradley release a virus into the world that would kill millions." Gwen sighed in disgust. "I should have known that he knew my real identity."

"Keep talking."

"By now Bradley must have contacted his brother...and his brother will contact my superior. His brother has the power to order my superior to terminate me," Gwen explained. "I speak the truth," she pleaded.

Amanda stared down into Gwen's panicked eyes. "Maybe you do," Amanda sighed. Unable to detect a lie in Gwen's voice or eyes, she stood up. "I—" Amanda began to speak but was interrupted when the phone on Sarah's desk rang. Amanda bounced up and grabbed the phone. "Sarah?"

"It's me," Sarah said, relief evident in her voice. "I—"

"I've caught myself a little spy," Amanda interrupted. "She was waiting in your office when I arrived. But she's been shot and claims that Bradley Preston is the culprit. Her name is Gwen."

Sarah drew in a deep breath and then told Amanda all about finding the tracking device, the listening device, and the canister. "Keep that woman in my office and stay put," she ordered.

"I will, and—" Amanda froze. A loud crash echoed from the rear of the coffee shop as the heavy back door slammed open so violently it banged into the wall.

"What was that?" Sarah asked.

"I think someone just kicked in the back door," Amanda whispered.

"My gun," Gwen pleaded.

Before Amanda could reach for Gwen's gun in the top drawer of Sarah's desk, the office door was kicked open, too. Bradley Preston stood in the doorway with his hired killer by his side. "Hello, again," he said. He snatched the phone away from Amanda and held it to his ear. "Detective Garland, I presume?"

"Detective Spencer and I are driving back now."

"Very good," Bradley said in a pleased voice. "You spoke to Mr. Pence?"

"Yes," Sarah admitted. Amanda, her heart racing as she strained to hear her friend's replies, silently prayed that

Sarah and Conrad still had a trick up their sleeves. "You knew we would," Sarah continued, "And we know you've been listening."

"Actually," Bradley said, sounding disappointed, "the device planted inside your Subaru has failed to work. That's the way of it sometimes."

"Please, Mr. Preston," Sarah said in a careful tone, "I know you have your agenda, but so do we. When Detective Spencer and I spoke with Mr. Pence, he told us about Gwen, Gregory, and Edward. We know they killed Charlie Raymond. I'm asking you to let Detective Spencer and me bring them to justice."

Amanda almost held her breath, struggling to keep her expression blank. Was this Sarah's plan?

Bradley only regarded Amanda with a pleased expression, apparently satisfied by Sarah's polite request. "I admit," he said to Sarah, "I may have been a bit hasty in my actions. But you must understand we are dealing with three very dangerous people."

"I know," Sarah replied. "Please, Mr. Preston, Amanda said one of them is in my office as we speak. Will you hold her until we return?"

"Gwen was my last target," Bradley informed Sarah. "I have eliminated the other two. But perhaps we can work something out. I can understand your hunger for justice and you can understand my position. So, let's make a deal," he offered with a cold smile "When you return, park the Subaru in front of your delightful little coffee shop so I can plainly see your arrival and then come around to the back with Detective Conrad."

"Will you turn the woman over to us?" Sarah asked.

"No," Bradley answered firmly, "but I will offer you an exchange. I can supply you with information on a certain Mr. Pence that will more than satisfy your hunger for justice."

"I...I'll..." Sarah started. "Yes, okay, Detective Spencer and I will meet you at my coffee shop. I'll call when we arrive in town."

"Very good," Bradley said and ended the call.

As he began to set the phone down, Amanda grabbed the kitten off the desk and threw it at Bradley so it landed squarely on his face. As the kitten's needle-sharp claws dug painfully into his skin, Bradley roared and stumbled backward into his henchman. Amanda snatched the kitten back, then charged forward like a linebacker and slammed into Bradley as hard as she could with her shoulder. Both men fell to the floor. Amanda jumped over them, hauled butt out of the office, and ran right into the barrel of a gun. A deadly-looking man wearing a black ski cap shook his head at her in warning. Amanda frowned, panicking anew, and slowly backed up into the kitchen.

"Put her in the office with Gwen," Bradley snapped to the man in the ski cap, getting to his feet. He mopped at the traces of blood from the kitten's claws with evident disgust. "We'll deal with her later. Right now, we have to prepare for the arrival of Garland and Spencer. I want them both dead."

CHAPTER NINE

Sarah's Subaru drove down the dark, snow-covered main street of Snow Falls and came to a stop in front of the dimly-lit coffee shop. The Subaru's headlights snapped off and the driver's side door opened. A man wearing Conrad's black coat got out and quietly closed the door. A woman wearing Sarah's coat opened the passenger's side door, climbed out and pointed at the side of the coffee shop. The man nodded his head and began walking. The woman followed.

Bradley watched this scene from a closed hunting gear shop across the street and spoke into his walkie-talkie. "Our two targets are on their way." He peered around the mannequin in the front display window. "Get ready."

"We're ready," a voice crackled over the speaker in reply. "Mitch and I are on the roof. We'll have one clean shot apiece."

Bradley watched the man and woman disappear around the side of the building. Lowering the walkie-talkie in his hand, he waited. The journey had been difficult and tedious, but here he stood, poised to claim his victory. Just outside, attached to the underside of the snow-covered Subaru, was his treasure. He had eliminated Charlie Raymond for capturing him speaking with Gwen, Gregory, and Edward in a photo—a photo which, if ever placed in the hands of the FBI or CIA, could have been extremely damaging.

Charlie Raymond was dead and the photo destroyed. The virus had even been delivered ahead of time—which was unexpected, but he had managed to finagle two errand boys to go and fetch his virus and return it safely. The only task that remained on his list was the elimination of those troublesome Snow Falls residents who had found themselves in the wrong place at the wrong time. Sarah and Conrad would come first, though. They knew too much, therefore they posed the most danger to him and had to be taken out.

Bradley waited, focused on Sarah's Subaru. And then, out of nowhere, two teenage kids appeared, running down the street. As he watched, they stopped in front of the coffee shop and began breaking into the Subaru. Before he could act, one of the boys managed to get the driver's side door open, jumped in, and reached down to hot wire the ignition while the second boy climbed into the passenger seat. Bradley, panic-stricken, ran for the front door of the hunting shop. The door was locked. “No!” he yelled and began kicking the door. “Out front, go...two kids are stealing the Subaru!” he screamed into the walkie-talkie.

At Bradley’s command, the two hitmen left their hidden position at the back of the coffee shop roof and ran to the front to peer down into the street.

Conrad watched them leave their position. “Go,” he said urgently to Sarah.

With her heart racing, Sarah ran to the back door of her coffee shop, unlocked it, and slipped inside while Conrad kept watch. “Amanda!”

“In the office!” Amanda yelled.

Sarah ran to her office and found Amanda on her knees, her hand on the forehead of a strange woman. “Let’s move. We have no time,” Sarah pleaded.

“I’ll be back for you,” Amanda promised Gwen.

“Go,” Gwen urged. Amanda handed Gwen her gun from the drawer, then ran out of the office with Sarah. “You sure took your time.”

“So sue me,” Sarah said as they burst out into the snowy alley.

“Okay, let’s go,” Conrad said. He offered Amanda a quick smile. “Good to see you.”

Amanda reached out and hugged him. "I'm glad to see you, too."

Sarah pointed to the end of the alley. "We need to move." She took Amanda's hand. "From now on, we're partners, understand?"

Amanda hugged Sarah as tight as she could. "You bet," she said.

"Let's move, ladies," Conrad ordered. He silently made his way up the alley.

In the dimly-lit street in front of the coffee shop, Bradley had just managed to escape the shop where he had been hiding, and he raced into the street with his gun drawn. He charged over to the Subaru's open door and pointed his gun into the face of the startled teenager at the wheel.

"Get out!" Bradley yelled.

"Hey we were just having a little fun," the redheaded kid said, throwing his hands into the air.

Bradley grabbed the kid, pulled him out of the car and threw him down into the snow. "You," he yelled at the blond-headed boy who sat frozen with fear in the passenger's seat, "take a walk or die."

"Okay, okay. I'm going!"

Bradley watched the redheaded boy scramble to his feet and run off down the street with his friend. "Get back into position," he hissed, waving angrily up to the two men on the roof. "Report," Bradley demanded into his walkie-talkie, kicking the door of the Subaru closed.

"Alley is...clear," came the response.

Bradley's face contorted with rage. "Get inside, now!"

Seconds later, he heard a barrage of deadly gunfire echoing in the shop. And then, silence. "Report!" Bradley yelled into the walkie-talkie. "Report to me now!" he yelled into the receiver again. But no report was given.

Throwing down the walkie-talkie, Bradley dropped down into the snow and crawled under the Subaru. Furiously, he searched for the silver canister. "There you are," he said as his fingers touched the old metal thermos.

Sarah stood and watched until Young Derby and Thomas Mitchell ran past the end of the building she was standing beside. Young spotted Sarah and sprinted over to her. "You owe us big time," he said, breathing hard. "That man had a gun."

"It was either that or jail time for breaking into the bakery," Conrad reminded them.

"Remind me never to owe you a favor again, Mr. Spencer," Thomas said wryly.

"Go home, gentlemen," Conrad said sternly as he pulled out his gun. Young and Thomas looked at each other and took off into the night.

"You two think you're clever Yanks, don't you?" Amanda said, hugging her arms. "I need my coat."

Conrad quickly took his coat off and wrapped it around Amanda. "Get to the station. Andrew is waiting there. He has orders to stay with the park rangers."

Sarah bent down and pulled her gun out of her ankle holster. "We're going to end this," she promised Amanda.

Amanda drew in a deep breath of cold Alaska night. Even though it had stopped snowing, she still felt like she was in the middle of a storm. "All this began when the dead body of a park ranger was found," she said sadly. "And will you look at the mess that has followed."

"Charlie Raymond deserves justice," Sarah said. She patted her friend on the shoulder. "You've been amazing through all of this. I promise, our next adventure is chocolate and a romantic comedy with a box of tissues."

Conrad eased his head around the corner of the building and looked down the dark street. He spotted Bradley pulling the metal thermos out from under the Subaru. "Let's move," he told Sarah.

Amanda watched as Sarah and Conrad began making their way down the street, hugging the front of each building, remaining in the shadows.

Bradley, unaware that Sarah and Conrad were closing in on him, studied the metal thermos in his hand.

Something wasn't right. "No...no...no...!" he shouted as the truth struck him. "No!"

"Hands up!" Sarah yelled at Bradley from the shadowy doorway where she stood.

Conrad dropped to one knee and aimed his gun at the British man. "One move and it's over for you, Bradley!"

Bradley threw his eyes toward the dark buildings. He spotted Sarah and Conrad holding him in the sights of their guns. "How did I get myself into this?" he asked himself in a melancholy voice, dropping the metal thermos. "I have diplomatic immunity," he called out loudly. He exhaled into the cold night air, the white cloud of his breath dissipating as the brutal chill stole his body heat with cruel fingers. "It would be wise to realize that you can't win this battle."

"Get your hands in the air," Conrad yelled. "Now! And tell your goons on the roof to come down and put down their weapons."

"My goons are obviously dead," Bradley informed Conrad in a dull tone, staring into the shadows. "Clearly, I underestimated the young woman I left wounded in your office, Detective Garland."

"Hands in the air," Conrad warned again. Bradley slowly raised his hands.

Amanda, who had watched Conrad and Sarah go with a

terrible feeling of dismay in her gut, crept toward them, watching Bradley. Her instincts were screaming that something terrible was about to happen.

"You're under arrest," Conrad said, keeping his gun aimed at the old man.

"You can't win," Bradley promised.

Conrad nodded his head at Sarah. She cautiously made her way over to her Subaru. As she did, a bullet ricocheted off the frozen sidewalk directly in front of her, and she stopped in her tracks. "Hands in the air," Gwen ordered as Amanda watched in terror.

Sarah looked past her Subaru and saw Gwen, her left arm in a sling, but her right arm very much functional. "She has a gun," Sarah warned Conrad.

Gwen came closer and aimed her gun directly at Sarah. "Drop your guns, both of you," she ordered, wincing only slightly as she cradled her bad arm to her side. "I only want the canister."

Sarah looked at Conrad. Breathing hard, she waited for his response. Conrad nodded his head and threw his gun down into the snow. Sarah followed suit. Gwen stumbled toward the Subaru, examined the snow around it, and spotted the metal thermos. She bent down and grabbed it. "Let's take a walk, Bradley," she said with cold satisfaction. "You two, get lost."

Bradley turned to Sarah and Conrad. "This woman intends to kill me. Are you going to allow that?" he asked, finally allowing fear to creep into his voice.

Sarah shrugged her shoulders. "Don't you want to hear what Gwen has to say, Mr. Preston? It seems only fair," she said with the barest hint of a smile. Just then she spotted movement behind Gwen. "Young lady?"

"What?" Gwen snapped at Sarah.

"Behind you!"

Gwen, looking in one direction, felt her other shoulder grabbed and she was pulled swiftly off-balance. The attacker spun her around and punched her directly in the face. Gwen stumbled back into Conrad, who quickly disarmed her. "And to think I once took pity on her," Amanda said, rubbing the knuckles of her right hand.

Sarah laughed—more out of relief than at her friend's humor—and hugged Amanda. "My hero," she said.

Amanda hugged Sarah back. "I need a holiday," she laughed.

Conrad grinned and looked at Bradley, who was eyeing the gun lying in the snow. "I wouldn't," he warned. Bradley met Conrad's eyes and stood very still.

Conrad kicked his feet up onto his desk. "Bradley and Gwen are in the custody of the FBI," he told Sarah and Amanda. "The British are anxious to get them back, too. And their little canister."

Sarah sat down in front of Conrad's desk, next to Amanda. "What will happen to them?"

Conrad shrugged his shoulders. "Who knows?" He looked at Amanda. "She probably knows."

"We won't ever see them again," Amanda promised Sarah. "Now," she said in a delighted voice, "what about tonight, Los Angeles? Are we still on for chocolate and a movie?"

"You bet," Sarah smiled. "I can't think of anything better. Conrad, you want to join us?"

"Nah," Conrad said, "I have some paperwork to finish up. You ladies go on ahead." He tapped a few keys on his computer and then frowned as he looked up to catch Sarah's eye.

Sarah stared into Conrad's eyes. "What's the matter?"

"Charlie Raymond's information has been erased from every single database...it's like the man never even existed. We can't charge Bradley because he's been deported back to the United Kingdom. We managed to stop a horrible terrorist attack, but...but Charlie Raymond didn't get the justice he deserved."

Sarah stood up and walked around the desk. "Conrad," she said, putting her hand on his shoulder, "I still think Charlie Raymond would be very proud of the justice that was served. We sent his killers to prison and captured a dangerous rogue agent."

"That's right," Amanda agreed. "Now, get up and come with us. We're going to eat chocolate, get fat, and watch a silly romantic comedy and cry some."

"I don't cry," Conrad said sternly.

Amanda nodded her head, stood up, walked to Conrad, grabbed his left ear, and yanked him up with a good-natured grin. "You will tonight," she said and pulled Conrad out of his office.

Sarah remained behind for a minute. She closed her eyes and saw the body of Charlie Raymond lying in the snow. "We did our best, sir," she said in a low voice. "I hope our best was enough for you."

"You coming, Los Angeles?" Amanda yelled from the hallway.

"I'm coming," Sarah called. She opened her eyes and looked out the office window. Outside, a gentle snow was falling, and far away, Diamond Lake was still frozen and sleeping peacefully. Another storm had come and passed, and Snow Falls was at rest once again. "I'm coming."

As Sarah walked out of Conrad's office and closed the

door, the phone on the desk rang. In New York, a scared man was standing at a rainy phone booth. “Come on, old friend, pick up,” the man begged. “Pick up...” Then gun shots rang out, and all that could be heard was the sound of falling rain.

ABOUT THE AUTHOR

Wendy Meadows is an emerging author of cozy mysteries. She lives in "The Granite State" with her husband, two sons, two cats and lovable Labradoodle.

When she isn't working on her stories she likes to tend to her flowers, relax with her pets and play video games with her family.

Get in Touch with Wendy
www.wendymeadows.com

amazon.com/author/wendymeadows
goodreads.com/wendymeadows
bookbub.com/authors/wendy-meadows
facebook.com/AuthorWendyMeadows
twitter.com/wmeadowscozy

ALSO BY WENDY MEADOWS

Maple Hills Cozy Mystery Series

Nether Edge Mystery Series

Chocolate Cozy Mystery Series

Alaska Cozy Mystery Series

Sweet Peach Bakery Cozy Series

Sweetfern Harbor Mystery Series

Candy Shop Mysteries

Made in the USA
Middletown, DE
31 January 2022

60122070R00076